We May Never Know

A Collection Of Bite-Sized Vignettes

Toyosi Temitope

Two Kobo Kollectif
Baltimore, MD

To those of us born with little

May we do much more than small

To those of us who dream often

May our dreams waltz into the sun

To those of us who seek freedom

May the wind reach us soon

To those of us who bear heavy silence

May ease find us all

These pages are borrowed from the corridors of reality

These words are written with the ink of imagination.

— Toyosi

There Is Space For All Of Us.

"Is it good enough? Is it interesting enough? Engaging? Long enough? Short enough? Literary enough? Who am I to do this? Am I good enough to do this? Is it simply, enough?"

These questions bullied me as I compiled these stories. Uncertainty and doubt were my companions through most of this journey. Add to that the fact that there are awesome works of writing in the world already. I mean, I have read works so amazing that I wanted to give up writing and simply remain a reader. Have you ever read a book so fantastic that when you flipped the last page and slapped it shut, you hugged it tight, whispering sweet nothings to it? I have had the pleasure of experiencing those moments of sheer decadence many many MANY times. But, although these amazing works exist, I remind myself of this truth "there is space in the world for your stories".

This is how I permit myself to do what I want to do, even with doubt gnawing at my insides and fear nipping at the seams of my confidence. I remind myself that there is space for my best and there is space for my worst as well

But the world can do nothing with what it is not given. So here is what I have to give. These stories, my imperfect work of art.

Maybe you sometimes struggle with doubt. Maybe

you think that what you have is not good enough. Maybe you want to wow the crowd and be excellent and incredible. And so, you wait and stall and push it forward, hoping for the day when it's all perfect or close enough to perfect.

And there's nothing wrong with this. But sometimes, imperfect is absolutely good enough. I'm no expert on life but I think that sometimes, the world becomes impatient and tired of waiting for perfect and it moves on, and accepts the realities of the imperfection it can have, leaving behind empty promises of perfection. We are imperfect humans in an imperfect world. We might not get it right the first time but that's what tomorrows are for.

I hope this book serves as a reminder of your permission to claim your space in our galaxy. There is space in our imperfect world for your most imperfect efforts. If it matters to you, imperfect as it may seem, out here in our amazing galaxy, it will matter to someone else too. Stop waiting. Put on your walking shoes and meet your dreams halfway.

Do it. Do it now. Do it soon.

Life is not forever.

There is space in our world for you, for me, for all of us.

Get on with you!

All my love,
Toyosi Elizabeth Temitope

We

May

Never

Know

P.S. Expect a LOT of imperfections within these pages!

We May Never Know

So here we are
Standing at the intersection of indecision
Pacing at the crossroads of uncertainty
Passing our weight from one foot to the other

Glancing furtively about
We long for the comfort of the familiar
We are wary of the uncertainty of the unknown
Yet we are weary of the routine of the same

Wringing the fingers of nervousness
We deepen the clutch of anxiety
Our stomachs fold in the palm of fear
"Should I or should I not?"

Unsure, we hang by the fragile cartilage of now
Swinging
Limbo
Limp

Until we decide to choose
The uncertainty of the future
Or
The satisfactions already past

Unsure though we are
We will go ahead still and try
Because if we try not
We may never know

1.

Road
Well
Traveled.

Road Well Traveled

This is no strange sojourn for me. I know this road well.

I've been down this road enough times to know how long it takes to get to the next bend with my eyes closed. Indeed, I've made enough journeys down this road with shuttered eyes to be familiar with every bump on it, every curve of it, every grind and thread of it. Back and forth on the same unending journey, undulating in this tightening whirlpool of events that seem to be choking me, yet I don't want to be free from it. Oh no. I choose to remain its freed slave.

Don't get me wrong, I'm not floating in some make-believe world of denial, rejecting the truth of my reality. No. No one in my shoes could possibly feign ignorance of the rawness of this blister I nurse. No one can be numb enough to. The throbbing ache and the heavy pain, the dizzying blows/ and the spinning smacks are all faithful agents of truth, slamming their reality into my consciousness, week after week. The cuts and the stitches weave jagged tales of technicolor, chronicling the fabric of my life.

I know this is misery but this is misery sweet and sour. It is strange, I know but it is a strangeness bearing familiar comfort and I embrace it as such. Just like a sad song, when you first hear it, you hate it and you just want to turn it off. But wait. Listen just a while longer. Ssshh. Just listen. Don't reason or judge. Just you listen. Do you feel it yet? Do you hear it? The subtle wisps of rhythm reaching out and parting the curtains of resistance. Can you hear it yet? That gentle caress of melody milked from its melancholic strain. And before you know it, you have that same song in a loop, replaying in your head and grazing your lips like the sour taste of an escaped expletive.

Survival.

This is the only weapon I have. This is the only weapon I can wield. Sticking it out. All the weapons of defense I can fashion are two-edged, this one included. Yet, I will very well nurse the cut of a familiar blade than the strange slash of an unknown one.

"Baba omo l'olomo."

If I leave, I will lose the children we've raised and everything we've built over the years. He will proudly remind me that when I married him, I brought nothing into his home and therefore, I would leave with nothing as well. Empty-handed and profit-less. After my many years of toil, what wisdom is there in leaving all the fruits of my many years of labor for another woman to reap? And then, what? What do I do? Start all over again? Where will that start be? What start is there to begin again?

This is all I've known my whole life. How do I unlearn half a lifetime's worth of learning? My husband can have a new wife before my shadow disappears through the door. But, who will take me? What love is out there for me, middle-aged and after-five me? That unfamiliar blade will not only slash me, it will severe me. Rip me into irretrievable pieces of what I fear to think about. No, please. I'll stick with the certainty and relative security of the familiar. Thank you very much.

Survival.

Don't worry about me. I've survived thus far. I'll survive further. The first cut is always the deepest, correct? Well, I'm already years from my first cut. Yes, it has never healed but it's not as deep as it used to be. Time heals all things, right? And if it does not, at least it brings somesort of smarting familiarity that can sometimes be comforting.

I know this road very well and I am not changing lanes. Its lines are engraved into my skin and its paths are etched into my palms.I will travel it until all its lights blink-blink-blur into darkness before my dimming eyes.

.a.

may the spring in your steps never slacken to
a drag
may the tilt of your chin never snap into a
sink
may the rise of your shoulders never fall in
weariness
may the straightness of your spine never
crumble in defeat
may the beam of your smile never wane
may the joy in your heart never wear
may the glint in your eyes never dim

yes, you may fall
but may you always rise
yes, you may lose your way
but may you never wander too far from home

yes, you may be hurt
but may you always find healing
yes, things may be hard sometimes
but may you always recover

may life never break your spirit
may life never defeat you
may you never know true loneliness in this
world

Amen.

2.

Alone.
Together.

Alone. Together.

The music was jamming when Kate arrived at Bogobiri House that particular Tuesday evening in June. She was at *Taruwa*, her favorite spoken-word poetry and live music hangout in Lagos. It was sort of her thing, her little fortnightly ritual every other Tuesday at 6pm.

Unlike that Tuesday evening, usually, she would get to Bogobiri House at 5:30pm, about half an hour before Taruwa started so that she could indulge in the artistic rawness of the place. It was how she pampered her senses after spending long working hours in the cold womb of her high-rise office with its sharp edges, glass surfaces, and clinical perfection.

The warmth of art and earth in Bogobiri House was the cure that purged her of the cold steel injected into her by her cold office. She would browse through the quaint gift shops with their many artsy offerings and buy a handful of knick-knacks here and there; she would go up the winding wooden stairs that led to the library with its many piles of tumbling books for a deep drag of that mouth-watering musty smell of aging memorabilia and flip through their pages, adding her fingerprints to those of the many other people who had held them before her; she would walk down the hallway gallery with art standing sentinel along its walls, stopping often to ponder the lines of one artwork as her eyes wandered to the enthralling texture of its neighbor's. At the end of the hall was the music store and she would browse through the wide collection of classic music, just to soak up the history in their vinyl plates.

Oh! and there was also the boutique hotel, that perfect pocket of escape from the madness of the city. It was a rustic haven with a modern blend. With its beautiful eclectic infusion of rich color tones, art, bamboo, raffia, pebbles and local fabrics into its decors, it was refreshingly different from the other shiny hotels in town. It was her favorite part of Bogobiri House. There was just something sensual about the place that pulled Kate there every time.

That Tuesday in June, she was late. She was never late. Okay fine, maybe never was an exaggeration but where Taruwa was concerned, she was always on time. But that day, she had been forced to work late at the office because of some last minute client concerns and she had left the office at 6pm, when rush hour traffic was at its beastliest on Mobolaji Bank Anthony Way.

"Better late than absent", she thought as she wrestled her way through the crazy traffic with the notorious Lagos danfo drivers. She was still fuming from being bullied by an especially crazy danfo driver when she finally made it to Bogobiri House. But as she stepped into the premises, the mellow sound of soft Afrobeat wrapped around laughter and friendly chitchat nudged her lips into a smile. The familiar ambiance distracted her from her angst and she walked towards the music.

There was a feeling that came with entering Taruwa. An almost imperceptible shift, so subtle that the transition could be easily missed. It was an experience in which the senses sensed differently. Kate always looked forward to that shift. The air seemed a bit different in there. The people with their liberated laughter and bold eccentricities; the drinks; the sounds; the tapestry of the people and the place. Things seemed just a little bit different in there than outside those doors. And there was also the smell. It was not a particular smell. It was a glorious, heady mix of both strong and soft smells, concocted from the aroma of oils in nappy hair, mixed with the whiff of melted butter on warm skin; the whisper of cigarette smoke clinging to clothing, mingled with the musk of body heat; all twirled around the smell of alcohol and spicy food drifting from the sidebar. It was a mouthwatering cocktail of welcome.

The room was packed with the usual suspects, their eccentric hairstyles creating a familiar outline across the room. There were vast puffs of afros, cute clusters of bantu knots and beckoning fingers of braids and dreadlocks in many different styles. Kate scanned the room, hoping for an empty seat or any available space to wiggle into. She spotted and hurried towards a seat just as Bibi, the emcee, announced the next act. Grateful for the seat, she hurriedly squeezed in between two guys, beaming a charming smile that made them create even more space for her.

The performer strummed a mic-check so deliciously melodious that fingers went snapping across the room. She had been too busy wiggling into her seat to hear his name when Bibi introduced him but she knew it was going to be a wonderful compensation for her lateness. He was one of those acoustic-soul-type artists, you know, those who performed with just their guitar and their voice, causing sheer awesomeness to happen. Just like two lovers and the love that binds them. Acoustic performers who strip their music and themselves free of frills. There was a rawness about them, a giving without holding back which gave their music such soul. As he adjusted the mic, Kate saw him clearly. He had a full beard and a head of dark locs packed into a loose bun. He was wearing loose-fitting linen pants with a matching white cotton shirt gently kissing his brown skin, a refreshing glass of difference from the way-too-many men she had seen that day in way-too-tight suits. There was a twinkling black stud earring in his right ear and a single fluttering feather swinging from a leather strap hanging from his neck.

She liked what met her eyes and ear and she had a feeling she was going to enjoy this one. The lights in the room dimmed, leaving only a soft blue spotlight on him and from the very first note of his performance, Kate knew she'd been right. He did a cover of 'I Am Ready For Love' by India Arie. He sang with such heart, Kate had goosebumps kissing her skin. The music was beautiful but the melody! Oh the melody of his voice did things to her insides. He had effortless control over his voice, riding the melody to a towering pitch and coming right back down to a vibrating baritone. She felt like a feather swirled into a slow waltz by the soft flirting fingers of a gentle evening breeze. She was enraptured by the soul in his voice, the fluid movement of his fingers on the guitar strings and the passion in his eyes as he sang. She could not tear her eyes off him.

Kate was in love with the man, his guitar, and his music. She was glad that the lights were dim because, with the way she was connecting to the music, she was sure her eyes were mirroring what she was feeling. She could practically taste the emotions in her own eyes.

As he continued his performance, his eyes roved from one face in the crowd to another, pushing the depth of his music even deeper with his soft passionate eyes. His eyes gently grazed hers and he lingered a bit with a soft hint of a smile tilting the right-corner of his lips. Kate smiled back softly, sinking deeper into her seat. He eyes roved the room again and then the strangest thing happened. His eyes came back to hers again and this time, he wouldn't look any-where else. At first, she thought he'd rove again but then he didn't. When he didn't, she tried to look away but as with the touch of a welcome company, she didn't want to break the contact. And then, with subtle ease, it seemed like every other sound in the room began to recede into the background- the clink of glasses as waiters served drinks at the sidebar, the chitchat of friends sitting together, the constant jiggling of the car keys of the guy sitting beside her, even her own breathing. Everything seemed to gently fade out and in that moment, with their eyes still locked like they were drinking oxygen from each other, it felt like they were the only people in that room. In the world. It felt like they were both performing for each other; he with his music and she with her silent attention, the soft spotlight on them both. They seemed suspended in timelessness, all alone in a world with just them two.

As the last note of his performance faded into the night, there was a split second silence, like the crowd was unsure whether he had fin-ished. In that second, everything seemed to zoom back in and a resounding applause rocked the room. The soft feather that was Kate was gently escorted down from the high that the gentle wind of him had taken her up to. As the applause waned, he stepped off the stage and moved towards Kate. Paralyzed by a heady mix of excitement and uncertainty, heart pounding, she breathlessly watched him approach her. He reached in his pocket on getting to her, pulled out a handkerchief and gave it to her. She took it and dabbed the tears she hadn't even known were there. It had the lingering smell of Smart Collection No. 28, that mouth-watering cocktail of freshness, like a mix of fresh lemons and the earthy musk of a man.

*****

Kate never saw him again.

Nobody ever did. No one seemed to be able to find him. But she kept the handkerchief as a souvenir of their encounter. A reminder that what happened was not just her imagination, the fading fragrance on the handkerchief a whisper of nothing in particular but of everything that had been that Tuesday night in June.

Alone. Together

.b.

each life is a different song
we all don't have to swing to the same rhythm
we may all listen to the same tune
but we all don't have to sway
to the same melody

3.

It
Was
A
Good
Day.

It Was A Good Day.

Papalolo stepped gingerly on the makeshift pako bridge laid across the brimming gutter in front of his house. It wobbled under his weight. He carefully shifted his feet apart, spreading his weight evenly to avoid tilting the pako in any one direction and risk tumbling into the gutter. He shook his head and spat with disgust into the brimming scum of the gutter. He shuffled carefully across until he got to the safe end and stepped off carefully. At last! On safe solid ground again! This careful shuffling was his daily routine if he was to leave his house The gutter was too wide for his old limbs to survive a sprint across; that was sport for the young now. The pako was his access to the world outside his door. He shook his head again and shrugged. At least, he had a pako to help him get across the gutter. he thought. The neighborhood rogues had either not seen it yet or did not value it worthy of their criminal expertise. He remembered when the last pako, and every other pako before it, had been 'moved' by the rogues. He had been left practically handicapped and at the mercy of his neighbors with whom he shared the 14-room face-me-I-face-you building, who had to flank and drag him across the gutter whenever he needed to go out of his house. His kind neighbors had also gone scouting for the sturdy pako which had been 'moved' and they had found it gracing the gutter in front of one of the houses on the notorious Saliu street, the street right across from their house. Their valiant efforts to repossess the pako led to a mini-battle and they had returned empty-handed and bruise-faced, defeated by the thieves on Saliu street who had used home advantage against them. After that, it was apparent they had no choice but to settle for the miserable wobbly pako which they had earlier abandoned after getting the now stolen one.

Papalolo slid his hand into the right pocket of his trouser and felt the papery dryness of his Voter's Card. He slid his hand deeper, picked out his kolanut and tucked it in the right corner of his mouth. It dangled precariously like it was going to tumble out at the slightest provocation yet, it remained snugly perched in his lip corner. He snipped at it and smiled.

It was going to be a good day. It was going to be the day that his voice would matter in the grand scheme of things in Nigeria.

He was a regular panelist at the local vendor's daily diagnosis of the state of the nation. His was a familiar voice in the chorus of hoarse men engaged in endless arguments and bitter protests, the snip-snip of his teeth clipping bits of kolanut often peppering his rhetoric. The past four years had held some of their most intense debates at the vendor's stand, all of which had made no difference in the continued decay of the system. It all ended as mere words falling to the ground like dead flies right there at the vendor's stand. But today was going to be different, he told himself again. Finally, he could do just one thing that would be louder and more impactful than all the many years of futile protests combined. With just one quiet action, his voice would indeed be heard. With a simple resolution in his heart to take one action, he would be speaking loud and clear, his voice ringing across Nigeria's six geopolitical zones, echoing the very same desire of millions of fellow compatriots. Today, all men would speak for themselves.

Papalolo was a believer. He believed in the constant need to try and try and try again until change happened. He believed that he was the 'one'; that extra one needed to unseat bad, unsatisfactory leadership and instate a better one. He was the difference that would give the right candidate that extra edge to win. Oh yes! He was the difference and he was determined to make that difference, wobbly pako or not.

He looked up towards the polling center on Saliu street, right ahead. The view pleased him. He could see the queue of voters, snaking out from the polling booth into the street. His people were changing and that was a welcome change. They were learning and he was glad. Unlike in previous election years when they would all refuse to go out and vote, complaining that *'we already know who go win so wetin be the need?'*, this time was different. It was a good day indeed. He smiled and snipped at his kolanut.

> *"Papalolo!"*
> *"Papalolo, you dey go vote?"*
> *"Vote for two o Papalolo"*
> *"The Only Papalolo"*

He waved at the okada riders who hailed him as they sped through the pot-hole infested street. Some of the okada riders were kai-kai addicts. They drank kai-kai on a normal day but on a day like today, heavy with tension and expectation, they had an extra reason to indulge even more. Some were in high spirits already because they had successfully sold their votes for a 'good' price while others were in surly but 'high' spirits still because they did not have their voter's cards to present as receipt to 'collect' from vote buyers, both groups just as dangerous. One had to be very careful crossing the street at such times. There were too many high spirits operating vehicles, too many chances for accidents, especially for a shuffling old man like himself, who had been stripped of his sprint by age and given a shuffle instead. To be fair though, sometimes, the accidents were caused by the gaping potholes which swallowed the tires of unsuspecting okadas. He looked down at his old feet. They were already covered in a generous coating of red dust rising off the street and clinging to the sheen of his vaselined shin.

It Was A Good Day.

He looked right, then left and then right
again to be sure that there were no speeding okadas approaching before he attempted to cross over
to Saliu street. He crossed the dusty street safely
to the junction of Saliu street and with a sigh and
another snip of kolanut, began the descent toward
the polling center. He pulled out his voters card and
gently rubbed his fingers across it.

"Today, we make history," he whispered to
himself.

He already knew who he was going to vote
for and no matter what the hooligans loitering the
polling center offered or taunted him with, he was
not changing his mind. He was going to vote for the
one candidate who had promised change in an area
that was especially personal to him.

*****

Papalolo had been a teacher at the Federal
Government Boys College, Ojo for thirty-five years.
When he turned 65, the retirement age, he had been
required to retire and he had done so gladly, after
many fruitful years of service and impact on young
lives. He had retired with bubbling hopes of ful-
filling his retirement dreams- to complete his cozy
bungalow in the village and relocate with his wife,
Mamalolo, to enjoy a life of peace and quiet. His
pension fund was the magic wand, the genie that
would make it all happen. But his anticipation had
waned into cold disappointment.

It Was A Good Day.

At first, he had been asked to wait for six months for the funds to be processed. Then it had turned to one year. And then two years of endless queues and fruitless appointments at the National Pension Commission. He had made friends with fellow pensioners on those queues, trading stories that ranged from the glory days of service to the bitter reality of the struggle which had brought them all together. He had also watched as familiar faces dwindled on the pension queues only to be replaced by a new batch of old faces every week. Friends made in solidarity died weekly, from sickness and simply being old, without reaping any rewards for all their years of struggle, and more new faces replaced them. And just like that, it had been five years since his retirement and his pension fund was still being 'processed', his retirement dreams in a gridlock of hibernation. Dark anger rushed to his head at the thought. His cozy bungalow still laid uncompleted in the village, a structural testament of his broken dreams. Even worse, he was still stuck in the crazy cycle of city life. Mamalolo had passed away a year ago after a heart attack. With no child or close family in the city, every day brought a greater desire to relocate from the madness of the city to the peace and quiet of the village. He was only getting by on the proceeds from the little provision store his wife had operated before she died.

However, he drew some comfort from the action he was about to take. The candidate he was voting for had promised to resolve the pension funds palaver, amongst other things. With carefully outlined strategies artfully communicated, he had won Papalolo and millions of other Nigerians. The contending candidate on his part was busy waving palm fronds (the representative symbol of his party) from one end of the country to another, spieling the stale and over-warmed promises that had become the anthem of elections in Nigeria:

"I will provide water. I will create jobs for the youths. I will repair roads. I will ensure constant power".

Shut your fufu trap my friend! Aren't there any intelligent young writers in that party who can craft good speeches?! Chai! Papalolo thought.

Even if his guy disappoints in office or fails to keep his promises, at least credit could be given to him for good presentation, confidence in delivery and conviction in communication. Anyway, there was no room for negative thoughts or doubts. It was decision day and there was no going back.

As he approached the polling station, he could hear what sounded like an argument brewing between the "sales reps" of the different parties. As he shuffled closer, the arguments heated up.

Papalolo got to the end of the line and joined the queue. *"Let me just vote and return to my house in peace"* he mumbled to himself, keeping wary eyes on the arguing reps.

They seemed to be trying to outbid one another in order to cajole the most number of voters

for their candidates. Suddenly, the argument erupt-
ed into a shouting match and one of the "reps"
punched the other in the face. Before anyone could
separate them, one of the fighting 'reps' looking
frantically around for a weapon of defense and
finding none grabbed the table where the election
officials were screening voter's cards and flung it
into the middle of the street. Chaos was unleashed.
Seemingly out of nowhere, groups of party-loyal
hooligans went rushing towards the polling center
brandishing machetes, broken bottles, clubs and
what Papalolo recognized as the wobbling pako he
had shuffled across just minutes earlier. It had become an impromptu weapon.

  Voters and election officials fled in different
directions, seeking safety as the youths turned Saliu
street into a battlefield. The two police officers on
duty quickly sought cover as well. They were out-
numbered and there was little only two of them
could do in the face of such mayhem. Ballot boxes
were smashed and voting sheets littered the street,
fluttering in the air like confetti at a carnival. Someone grabbed a bottle of kerosene from a nearby
seller's store and another pulled a log of burning
wood from beneath Iya Alakara's fireplace. In swift
motions, the ballot boxes and their contents were
set ablaze, along with other election materials. Papalolo was horrified and his heart fell as he watched
his hope for change burn before him. He had not
even gotten a chance to make his contribution.
What hope did he have now? What he did know for

sure was that he needed to find some form of safety. He shuffled as fast as his old limbs would go, heading towards home. He was close to the junction and could see his house just right across the street with no pako across the gutter. He was wondering how he would make it across the wide gutter when he felt a blunt strike against the left side of his bald head.

*****

The kolanut popped out of its perch as he stumbled and fell to his knees. A sharp ribbon of pain zapped from his head to his eyes. He reached behind his head to touch the assaulted spot and felt the sticky warmth of blood. It trickled down his neck and he felt faint. Hot fingers of pain shot through his bruised head and he fell with a hard thud on his chest. He felt a bit relieved, laying down there, dust rising all around him from the many feet running in the mayhem, his ears ringing from the roar of chaos as the fight raged on. He saw his voter's card laying just an arm's length away from where he laid. He reached for it but a pair of running feet landed close and the air from the impact blew it beyond his reach. Papalolo was weak, his eyes were growing dim, the roar of chaos was beginning to fade into a muted hum. He saw his voter's card fluttering away on the dusty wind, in the midst of the raging chaos.

Then, a numbing darkness.

muted hum. He saw his voter's card fluttering away

on the dusty wind, in the midst of the raging chaos.

Then, a numbing darkness.

.c.

let us make fufu, not bombs!
let us make egusi, not hate!
let us throw a feast, not grenades!
let us throw an owambe, not shells!
let us make babies, not soldiers!
let us make love and not war!

4.

A
Higher
Hand.

A Higher Hand.

Nneka squirmed, trying to find a comfortable position for her knees. She moved her weight from one knee to the other. She had been kneeling for almost twenty minutes, the cold concrete floor pushing up against her burning knees. Her knees hurt but her heart hurt even worse. She wanted so badly to look up into the faces of those gathered around her; gathered because of her; but she had been vehemently warned to keep her head down as a sign of remorse and not to so much as cross eyes with anyone, most especially Ugo, her husband. She could almost feel the megawatts of disdain singe her skin as her mother-in-law and sisters-in-law shot eyeballs of hate her way. They had never liked her much and had never bothered to disguise it, blaming her for being the poor wretched girl who dared to win the affection of their rich son and brother. Today was even more reason to hate her.

It had been over an hour of back and forth between his family and hers. Accusations and counter-accusations had flown over her down-turned head. His family would raise accusations against her and highlight reasons why they would prefer that she continued to stay with her parents and left their son alone; her family would appease them with palm-oil coated proverbs to counter their points. The back and forth was impressive and heated. Were the circumstances different, Nneka would have enjoyed the negotiations.

Eventually, there was a break in the back and forth. Her husband's kinsmen conferred in a cluster for a while in muffled high-low whispers, many heads shaking sharply and hands cutting the air swiftly in gestures of disagreement. After a while, the spokesman for her husband's people peeled from the group and stood in the middle of the room. He cleared his throat and said, "It is apparent that there is wisdom in this family. With your wise use of proverbs and your well-salted words, you have wrestled the fight out of our hands. Despite our grievances and anger, you have proven to be an amiable opponent, using your charming manner to take down our weapons of quarrel. It is however, surprising that from such a fountain of wisdom, a river will still choose to flow without bearing the liquid of its source. My in-laws, to be brutally honest with you, we came here today with one singular intention- to end our union with you. Oh yes! Because we consider what Nneka, your daughter, did to our son, Ugo, a big insult to our family. Almost a

A Higher Hand.

sacrilege I tell you. Aru! Nobody will sit down
with folded arms and allow another person to
rub shit on his face. Mbanu! However, our people
say that when a person realizes his mistake and is
truly remorseful, it is only right to give the
person another chance. Even God our creator
forgives our grave offenses. We also must do
alike. Ehn, we have deliberated and decided to
give Nneka a second chance. We will welcome her
back as our own daughter and let bygones be
bygones. But only for this one time. We will not
tolerate a repeat of this and our forgiveness will
not be repeated either". He sat down amidst
murmurs of agreement from both families.

Nneka's family spokesman stood up,
beaming a smile of relief as he looked around
and said, "My in-laws, a lot has been said today
and I don't want to add to what has already been
said. We thank you greatly for your kind hearts
and forgiving spirits. We again apologize deeply
for this embarrassment and we pray that when
next we meet, it will not be for such as this but
for merriment and celebration. Words cannot
express how grateful we are. Thank you indeed.
Now, as a token of our remorse and regret for
this unfortunate situation and to truly be assured
of your forgiveness, we invite you to join us in a
little humble offering we have prepared for you.
Our daughter Nneka specially prepared the soup
to show her remorse as well. It is all to show
how sorry she truly is. Please join us in the

backyard and together, let us bury our grudge completely in thick globules of fufu and wash our anger with fresh palm wine. It is popularly said that only true friends and brothers share a meal of fufu and palm wine", he concluded amidst loud roars of laughter and nodding heads affirming his words.

It had been a long morning of talks. The invitation to eat was a perfect seal on the proceedings of the day. They all rose and moved to the backyard, brushing past her in her kneeling position in the middle of the room, ignoring her. Even Ugo, her husband walked past without a word; she knew it was him because that unique musk of him enveloped her as he walked past her and her heart did a little flip. She had actually missed him.

When the group had moved to the back of the house and the meeting room was empty, her mother called her to the kitchen to begin to serve her in-laws their meals.

*****

As she set about her serving duties, bearing trays laden with steaming bowls of fufu and egusi soup and chilled glasses of palm wine, she thought about the irony of it all.

They had all gathered because of her, yet she hadn't been allowed to look up or even say a word. Everyone kept apologizing on her behalf when, in truth, she wasn't actually sorry. But no one would let her speak anyway so they'd never know. No one seemed to care that he had choked her almost to an inch of her life and her response had only been triggered by her survival instincts. No one seemed to care that he had battered and bruised her countless times. No. They all pretended like they couldn't see the bruised impression of his fingers welted around her neck. No one seemed to remember that he had squeezed her neck but there was an uproar because she had squeezed his balls in retaliation. No one bothered to ask how and why they got there- him squeezing her neck and her clutching his balls. No one bothered to ask about such things anymore these days. They had stopped asking after the first few times. The whys and hows stopped to matter because they sounded too often like excuses for her to complain about her good husband. All anyone did nowadays was either to bully her into keeping her mouth shut or ignore her complaints (and bully her still) into apologizing to him. Anyway, even if they did care, what could they do? No one was going to berate or blame him for what he did or for all the many times he had done the same thing in the past. Neither was anyone going to tell her to leave. For where? Leave to go where na?

Of course she could not express all these thoughts. Who would listen to her wretched cry when money was roaring? What would it earn her but more scorn and labels of *"ungrateful wom-*

an who has a husband who is taking care of her but she still complains". There wasn't much anyone could do because no one could do anything to help her. Not even her parents. They could barely take care of themselves and couldn't bear to have her return home when she had a rich husband who lavished money on all of them. He had married her straight out of secondary school and she had no skill or business of her own. He had refused to let her work or start a business because he was rich enough to not need her help. She could not even help herself. It was almost laughable if it was not so pathetic.

Oh well, that was her sentence. All she needed to do was to be quiet, please him and just make him happy. Her silence would cost her, but that was the price she had to pay to avoid an uncertain future.

So she mechanically set to work, avoiding making eye contact with everyone. Wearing her most remorseful face, she curtseyed countlessly as she went from table to table, serving them all in her best manner.

She looked over at Obi. He was staring at the seductive ribbons of steam swirling up towards the ceiling from the bowl of egusi soup in front of him. He had not touched the food, a silent grunt of reluctant forgiveness. She had served him first, touching her already bruised knee to the sandy ground of the backyard as she placed the plates of food carefully in front of

him. But he had still not looked at her. That was
expected. He couldn't give back his forgiveness
too easily after the humiliating incident that had
dealt a blow to his manhood. He wasn't expected
to. He shouldn't. He had to save face with his
people and hers. So, he kept his eyes fixed on a
spot above her shoulders. Thankfully, he had not
tossed the meal off the table. Yet. She had heard
of husbands who flung the meals they were
served on such occasions off the table, a loud
voiceless roar of their bruised pride. She had a
strong feeling Ugo was not going to do that
though.

She saw his Adam's apple bop up and
down in a quick swallow. Ahh yes. It would only
be a matter of minutes before he would give in
to the seduction of the soup. Egusi was his
favorite soup, his Achilles' heel, and the special
aroma of the okporoko in the soup had formed a
delicious cloud of aroma in the evening air,
clinging to clothes and skin. It was an aroma too
delicious to ignore. The oil-rich yellow of the
egusi generously mixed in gorgeous contrast with
the leafy green of the ugwu and the rich brown
of the assorted meats in the plate was too beautiful to ignore. She was certain that his taste buds
were drowning in a sea of craving as he stared at
it.

As she headed back to the kitchen to grab
another tray of food, she saw him cut a generous
lump of fufu and crown it with the soup. She

quickly buried her chin in her chest to hide the smile of quiet victory tugging at the corners of her lips. As she did, she clapped eyes with Ugo's mother and seeing the dark questioning scowl on her face, Nneka fled into the sanctuary of the kitchen. Her shoulders were sore from carrying tray after tray of food to all of the people present. But she made no complaints and swallowed her suffering into silence. It was her punishment. She had offended the clan. She must pacify the clan.

When the merriment ended, they all left, fufu-filled and palm-wine pampered.

On his way out, speaking to her for the first time that day, his eyes still fixed above her shoulder, Ugo told her to prepare to return home the next day. And then he left, without another look in her direction.

*****

The next day, when he came to pick her up, her parents sat with him and prayed for him; long prayers masking their continued apologies. Then they turned to where she was kneeling, again, on the side.

"Nneka, you have bitten the finger that fed you," her father said.

"No o. She did not only bite the finger that fed her, she bit off the nipple that the whole community suckles from. You are ungrateful and selfish, thinking about yourself alone Nneka. But thank God for the hand of God in Ugo's life that he has so graciously forgiven you," her mother added.

"We cannot apologize enough Ugo my son but know that we are very sorry about this whole mess, o?" her father said.

*****

After another long session of apologies and accusations, she was released from her kneeling punishment to go gather her things, ready to return home with her husband. She went into her parents' bedroom to pick up her bags. As threads of their continued prayers for him filtered into the room to torture her, she slammed her eyes shut, trying to shut it all out for a few more seconds. She sighed at the pitiful image of her parents' effusive gratitude to him for not rejecting their daughter. In this one bedroom apartment, they had even much more than she would ever have in Ugo's five bedroom duplex.

*****

The silence in the car was heavy, both of them staring keenly ahead as the car pulled them from one fate into another. Only the soft purr of the car filled the silence.

Getting home, he got out of the car, slammed the door and went into the house, leaving her to lug her belongings into the house.

He was standing at the little side bar in the sitting room when she entered the house. She stood and stared in his direction, waiting for him to say something, anything, maybe a vocal permission for her to go ahead. He turned to the bar and picked up the glass of drink he had poured himself. As she walked towards the staircase leading to their bedroom, his voice halted her.

"I'm only going to say this just this one time. The two nonsense you tried with this past drama, grabbing my balls and running to your parents' house, don't you dare EVER try that with me again."

He turned back to his drink and Nneka dragged her unwilling feet and heavy heart to the bedroom.

It was certain dejavu.

It would only be a matter of time before it happened again.

.d.

You count. I count. We all count.
We are all important threads in the fabric of
life.
Equally important beads in the shekere of life.
You're an important piece of the crazy puzzle
of life.
You help me make sense of the world.
Your presence in life gives clarity to some di-
lemma that I'd otherwise be stuck in.
At the end of the day, all that we are all basi-
cally trying to do is to touch the world in our
unique ways.
We might not all change the world. We might
not all move the world. We might not all
shake the world.
But thank goodness we can all touch the
world.
Matter of fact, that's exactly what we all do.
Every one of us.
With our presence.

With our living and being.
With our works and words.
With our big things and small things.
With our presence in life.
We all touch the world.
With the bloody hands of butchers and
the tough hands of farmers
With the keyboard clicking hands of writers
and the package-lifting hands of factory
workers
With the knowledge-giving hands of teachers
and the expressive hands of dancers
With the threading hands of a tailor and the
hammering hands of a carpenter
With the cradling hands of mothers and the
comforting hands of fathers
With the navigating hands of drivers and
sailors and pilots
With the dough-kneading hands of bakers and
the drink-mixing hands of bartenders
With the gesticulating hands of speakers and
the coding hands of techies
With the caregiving hands of nurses and
doctors and caregivers
With the smooth hands of youth, reminding us
of new beginnings and fresh starts
And with the veined hands of age, reminding
us that life is worth living

*With hands that hold and let go and give and
take and push and pull
With hands that caress and punish and lift
and lay down
With hands that hug and twirl and squeeze
and pinch
With hands that lead and follow and repair
and separate
With hands that seduce and tease and invite
and satisfy
With a firm grip or a gentle caress*

*We all touch the world still.
In all that we do, we are all touching the
world in unique ways.
Yes.
What you do is important because if no one
does what you do, if you don't do your thing,
there will be a void somewhere in the world
and our world will miss it.*

*If our world was the story capital of the
galaxy, you and I would be the words and
lines and sentences etched across its pages.*

You count. I count. We all count.

5.

Eyes
Wide
Shut.

Eyes Wide Shut.

This is a silent cry for help, a help I need but I am afraid to receive.

My name is Pat and I am in a messy tangle.

Nighttime holds horrors for me. Unlike the ghoulish movie-type horror, this is a domestic horror that triggers no screams or bloodshed, yet it is as chilling, in its subtle creepy execution as any horror there is.

I am a teenage girl who was rescued from the claws of hunger and certain suffering by my aunty's husband, Uncle James. After my parents died, my Aunty and her husband took me into their custody, since there were no other family members willing to take responsibility for me. As an only child newly orphaned, I had no one else and she opened her home to me. They became my only remaining support in the world and I was grateful.

The horror started one fateful night with a touch. I woke up with a start. Had I imagined it? I sat up quickly and the soft sway of the curtains caught my eyes. If I had imagined it,

could I have also imagined the swiftly retreating
back of the disappearing shadow I just saw
sliding through the curtains? The curtains bil-
lowed softly again as if to convince me that I
had been imagining things. Or maybe they were
whispering hidden secrets, I wasn't sure. No! I
could not have imagined a touch so real or
dreamt such perversion. Never! I got off the bed
and slid my hand between her pajama-clad thighs,
to try and simulate the intrusion I was sure woke
me up. Nah! My senses registered right! Yet, I
still wasn't sure. Or maybe it was my heart holding on to a thread of hope that it wasn't true. I
laid back on my bed, eyes searching the dark for
answers, curled up into a sickening pot pourri of
emotions. Shame, disgust, dread, uncertainty, and
at my core was a knowing sadness.

A week later, I woke up to the strangest
sensation. I was floating in the fog of sleep but
the cloud was gently parting to bring me into a
most horrid discovery. My senses awakened one
after the other to this reality. My skin crawled in
disgust at the circling touch. My ears picked up
the controlled breathing. I could smell the des-
perate sweat and bile rose to my mouth as the
realization clicked. But my eyes, oh my poor eyes
remained wide shut, not wanting to behold this
horror. They were shut but in the darkness of
their shut lids, they could see all that sight
painted. Uncle James, my aunt's husband was in
my room. He was making circular movements

around my nipple with his finger. He tried very desperately to be gentle in order not to wake me up. His hands shook from the demanding effort to control his raging lust and channel it all into a gentle methodical touch. I lay there, eyes locked and limbs frozen in fear. And this act of inaction opened a vista of horror. Nightly horrors.

Some nights he would rub my buttocks; others, he would slip his finger through my pajama-bottom and worry my clitoris. And then, there were those extra horrid nights when he would not touch me but I would hear his heavy breathing in the shadows, as he heaved and huffed through many masturbation sessions in my room.

*****

I wasn't ready to confront the consequences of what this might mean so I bore the many nights of preying with a mix of silent fear and anger. Whenever he left, I'd cry myself to sleep. The lights dimmed in the world and the sparkle waned from living.

I was afraid. Not only by the thought of confronting him but also by the consequences of it. I was also hesitant to confront him because if I let him know that I knew, I would have to take a definite action- tell my aunty, risk her family falling apart and face an uncertain future myself or silently endure it for as long as I could. I didn't want him to know that I was afraid to tell my aunty because he could take advantage of that and continue his abuse even more brazenly, preying on my fear. He could also get brashly defensive about the threat of me telling my aunt and as a result, make my stay with them hell, just to frustrate me. He was after all one of those patriarchal types who believe that the life of a woman was owned by her husband and he ruled his home the same way. He would probably even threaten to send both I and my aunt away if I told on him, knowing we both had nowhere else to turn to. So I remained silent. Quietly breaking inside every other night when he strolled in and did as he pleased with me. I was in a dilemma and I was ashamed of my weakness. Many nights, I'd stay awake, pretending to be reading with the hopes that the light of my reading lamp would drown out his darkness. I even had a special alarm titled 'Watch and Pray' timed to go off hourly on those nights when I was too weak to keep awake by my will.

At first, he'd casually stroll by my room as he always did to see if the coast was clear. When he noticed that I had made this a habit, he complained to my sister about my unhealthy sleep habit and how he wanted everyone in his household to get quality sleep every night. In time, he started complaining about how the light from my room and the rustle of my books were somehow disturbing his sleep. His house, his rules. I was banished back into the slavery of the darkness.

I, born free of all shackles of slavery and fear picked up the shackle of silence and fear and bound myself with them. I, who was the champion of liberation through expression amongst other teenage girls in my neighborhood was now caught up in a web of uncertainties and indecisions. I, who strongly believed that a problem shared is half-solved now doubled my own wahala in my silence.

I devised several weird ways I hoped would beat him off without having to confront him outrightly. I would arrange as many of my books as I could on the bed to form a makeshift perimeter around me and curl up into a tight ball to await what the night held; sleep or something else. I did this with hopes that perhaps he might be dissuaded from trying anything with the heightened chances that I might wake up while he parted the books to reach me in the far corner of the bed where I'd scuttle to. This didn't work. He'd very methodically, rearrange my book-fortress and still reach for me. I also on a lot of occasions tried heavy breathing when I felt him close. This worked only temporarily because he would quickly exit my room but always returned. Sometimes he'd not even leave, he'd just simply back-off into the dark shadows of my room and wait for silence to return. I even feigned sleep-talking, sudden rustlings in my sleep to help move out of his reach but this man would only stiffen, wait to see if I'd fully wake up or quickly exit only to return a short while later. It felt like being stalked. I was baffled. Wasn't he even scared for once that I could wake up suddenly? Or his wife could walk in? This man was very alert. He was sensitive to every reflex in the house and he would swiftly exit into the kitchen if he heard the rustlings of his wife, pretending to be getting a midnight snack.

After several weeks of silent torture and misery, I confronted him for the first time. He apologized, said it was a mistake and even lied that it was the first time. He said he'd never do it again and I should give him a benefit of the doubt. I was too ashamed to confront him that I knew it wasn't the first time because I felt guilty and dirty for allowing it to go on for so long. But of course he continued to return and I continued to keep my nightly vigil. Sometimes, I wished I could just fall into the oblivion of sleep while it happened but it seemed I was afraid of what could happen while I was unaware.

I confronted him several times again and do you know the most ridiculous defense he gave? He told me that he only touched me and didn't do anything more and he wasn't even planning on doing anything more. Therefore, I shouldn't make such a big deal out of it. He said, "Nobody's perfect Pat, not me and surely not you; shit happens, deal with it! Everyone has shit to deal with. However, in dealing with our shit, we shouldn't create more shit for others to deal with by smearing shit everywhere".

Can you believe that?!

I was hurt! I was angry! Yet I was helpless because I had to think through whatever my action would be. Not because he said it but because of my aunt and her children. We had nowhere to go and I didn't want to put her through the misery of making the wrong choice. It seemed like it would be a never-ending loop and that scared me. My nights were marred by those all too familiar depressions on the edge of my bed, announcing his nightly visit. They marked the beginning of my nightly nightmares.

*****

I think about my mother and how she struggled with the many ghosts of my Father's infidelity for most of their marriage. How she nursed a deep bitterness from the choice she made to stick with him regardless because of me, their child; how she brandished me as a justification for her choice and a defense against the many hurts he threw her way. I weep every time I remember that familiar look in her eyes. That deep empty well of longing for love and faithfulness from the man she so dearly loved. And almost always, that longing would morph to spite very quickly. I weep even more at the memory of her etched in my mind- a woman deformed by the pain of her choice. I think about my aunt's little children who know nothing about the crazy spiral the world can take. I think about how this could throw them into a reality their little minds cannot grasp but one which might mar their lives forever. I think about the consequences of whatever choice I make. Will more people suffer if I tell than if I don't? Do I even have the privilege of choosing? Is this a situation of "it's your story and you can choose to share it or not" or "blood makes you related but loyalty makes you family"? How am I sure the table won't be flipped and I get the short end of the stick? What if, in true local character, I get the blame? Or worse still, what if nobody believes me? What if my aunty decides to leave him, doesn't that make me a home-wrecker? And if she chooses to stay, will there be spite and bitterness and most of all, won't she despise me? Do I want this for my aunt? I love her so dearly and I want to protect her from as much as possible. What will this do to her? Will it hurt her more than it helps her or vice versa?

Oh so many questions spilling out of my mind!

What should I do/
Or should I do nothing?

*****

I am writing this letter, not because I have made up my mind about how I will unravel myself from this tangle. I simply seek solace in the simple act of expressing the raging confusion in my mind and capturing my emotions through liberated words, hoping that my tortured mind does not cave under the pressure of its many musings. I am trapped in a loud silence with lips parted in a muted wail, a wail my heart gives but my mouth dare not voice because, how do I explain it? My eyes are wide shut at night, following the shifting shadows in the dark from behind my tightly shut lids. And my limbs, are frozen attachments to my screaming body, constant reminders of my active inaction. I am a prisoner of the choices I chose not to make and the ones I choose to make. I am also a prisoner of the choices I did not choose not to make.

.e.

we may forgive
we may move on
but sometimes
we do not forget
so that we may remember
not to repeat.

6.

Piecing
Broken
Pieces.

Piecing Broken Pieces

The buzzing in her ear seemed to play in an unending loop. It reminded her of the time, long ago, when she went for a carnival and the speakers had been terrible. They had been turned up so loud that it seemed they were wailing their poor broken metallic hearts out. So bad was the sound they emitted that she had been stuck with a constant static buzzing in her badly abused ears two days afterwards. Only difference was that this time, the buzzing was not caused by sound abuse. It was from a violent strike that left her half-deaf.

As it began to clear out, thoughts floated through her mind.

"I don't deserve this" the thought softly bounced off the walls of her mind. "I'm worth much more than this".

She went about mechanically cleaning the kitchen which had been the battlefield where she'd just been unfairly vanquished without much of a fight on her part. She bent to gather up the vegetables she had been preparing before he had come with the battle and flung them all over the floor with a violent sweep of his hand. The tomatoes were still rolling from side to side, the peppers were red hot sores all over the floor and the onions were bruised balls with flayed skin. At the point of picking up the last ball of bruised onion, she saw the blender laying broken in a far corner of the kitchen. Another victim of his violence, once whole and complete, it lay there now in pitiful shards of jagged glass, metal and plastic. From a wholesome life of proper functioning to one with its essential parts pieced apart.

It was the perfect metaphor.

She picked up the pieces of the blender and tried to piece them together but she soon realized that some tiny yet essential parts were missing. The blender had fallen to the ground a few times before in the past and it hadn't shattered. And then the light of realization pierced through her mind. It took constant falling and then that one fatal fall to crack even the strongest into pieces. She swept the tiny scattered pieces of the blender into a bin and wondered if one day her own life would be swept away.

It was a random, subconscious thought but it snapped her. And like one jolted by an electric charge, she dropped the dust-pan, turned round like a soldier doing the about-turn and headed out of the kitchen, out of the door, out of the house and off the battlefield. She was done! Done fighting the urge to fight back. Done giving in to the urge to hold back. Done giving in to the urge to give in. Done losing the many battles she never even fought.

Done!

She wasn't going to stick around till she was broken into unrecognizable pieces and swept into oblivion. She was going to strengthen all those parts of her that had cracked from her falls and move on, webbed as she may be by her battles, yet still WHOLE!

.*f*.

Hey you,
Have you met you lately?
You're incredible and beautiful
and sometimes,
words are inadequate to describe you.
Have you heard your jokes?
Have you listened to your conversations, the
way you weave words together
in your own special way?
Have you felt the passion of your love?
Have you searched your depths?
Have you heard the chorus of your laughter?
Have you seen the glint of mischief in your
eyes when you're up to naughtiness?
Have you seen the glow of your smile?
Have you met you?
You're amazing!
You're important and you matter.
Yes you!
You're hope in this present
time for those in the time to come.

SideBar

You're an important piece of
life's crazy puzzle.
You help me make sense of the world.
You're alive and you're living
and learning and growing
and becoming and making amazing
and making mistakes and doing just fine.
You're not perfect.
You're simply trying to be your best you.
And that?
That is perfect enough.
Stay awesome!

all my love.
toyosi

7.

No
More.

No More

Mine is like the story of the one whose beauty is her curse, a curse laid on me by my husband. At inception, it was a soothing balm of flattery to my inner goddess. Oh how warm and delightful it felt to be wanted and desired so. To hear him say 'I want you only to myself, for my eyes only, for my touch only, exclusively mine'. To see his customary sign-off phrase, 'Exclusively mine' in every note or text he sent me. It sure felt good to be wanted. If only I knew just how literally he meant it.

We met at a poetry bar about seven years ago. It was a place I frequented with my girls every Wednesday evening. It was our special spot to hang-out, gist and generally catch-up and keep in touch. I especially loved it because it was my haven of poetic expression. I was a closet poet until I discovered that bar. We had always had challenges with finding the ideal place to hang out and ideal for us meant good music, a relaxed, atmosphere and great people. We almost always changed our rendezvous spot every week because a sore thumb always stuck out in them. They either had terrible, terrible music, a crappy atmosphere or just plain scary people. Our least favorite was the scary people bit. You know how they say the freaks come out at night? Well, that statement is not far from the truth because mehn! freaks DO come out at night. We had our unfair share of encounters with them. So this place became a sort of oasis for us.

I and Tega, my husband, met the very first day I took the bold step up to the mic. I did a performance of my poem about being a woman. From that moment, the rest of the night and my life afterward took an amazing turn. Another poet went up after me and although I was deep in some juicy gist with my girls, only half-heartedly listening to the next poet. I snapped to attention when the point of his performance anchored its root in my mind. He was doing a sequel to my performance and his subject wanted a woman exactly like the woman I talked about in my poem. And boy! Did he do an amazing job! I was impressed. Everyone in the bar was impressed. We got talking afterward and well, we always seemed to have something to talk about all the time. We, after all, had a lot in common. He was a seductive wordsmith who was not afraid to use his ability to paint his feelings every chance he got. And he wooed me good!

We started dating three months later and three years later, we got married. We were perfect for each other. Well, we were as close to perfect as our imperfections would allow. There was, however, a niggling worry I had. He was possessive and really jealous. It was mild and frankly flattering when we were dating and I didn't mind in the least. But after we got married, it seemed to get worse. It became chronic jealousy and paranoia. Spending time with my girls was out of the question completely because he could not bear to have me out of his sight. He so much as got me a job in his office so we could practically spend every waking hour together. I had no excuse to be away from him.

He hit me for the first time because one of our bosses had complimented my new hairstyle. I didn't realize he had been offended by it. As I prepared for bed that night, I carefully arranged my hair and tucked it into my sleeping cap. He had been broody most of that evening and watching me from the bed, he spat bitterly "Why are you primping and paying so much attention to your hair? Oh it's because Mr. Alex complimented it abi?" I was shocked but I chuckled dryly and said he couldn't be serious. He skulked out of bed to where I was seated and smacked me across my face. I was so shocked that I fell off the dresser stool, sprawled on the floor. He climbed back into the bed and went to sleep. I could barely sleep that night.

He apologized the next morning. But that was the beginning of my nightmares. He gave me hell about my hair so much that he demanded I

cut it. Thankfully, I also loved being au natural
so I made the best of that. He stopped me from
wearing some of my dresses which he tagged
"too perfect". Eventually, he pressured me into
quitting my job and becoming a stay-at-home
wife. It was as if he didn't want to share me with
anyone. Not even my family and friends. I resort-
ed to lying and making excuses to cover up my
many absences.

One time, I invited my friends for drinks
at our home. He was out of town and I wanted to
catch up with my girls. None of them knew what
was going on because I believed that it would
pass eventually and I didn't want them to continue to see him as that same man, long after we
hopefully would have moved on from it. You
know how issues like this can be; people hold
grievances on your behalf, long after you might
have gotten over the grievances. I was afraid they
would probably never forgive him and continue
to judge him based on his past mistakes. So I
kept my nightmares to myself, hoping and pray-
ing for a sweet, liberating dawn.

*****

Well, somehow, he found out about our
little get-together and beat me to a painful pile.

Having him around was a carousel of
dread and misery. He didn't beat me all the time
but when he did, he did it good! Hearing the key
turn in the lock when he returned from work

every evening sent darts of fear through my heart. I was always grateful every time he left in the mornings and returned late in the evenings so that we spent less time together and thereby, he had fewer reasons to get mad about the most random things I did. But I loved him still. I wanted to stick it out, hoping it was just a phase that would pass. I didn't want to give up on him, on us. I wanted our marriage to work.

I never successfully pulled through a pregnancy because he knocked me up good and then knocked me free of them with his bashings.

My friends did not relent in keeping in touch and trying their hardest to get me to hang out with them. And it turned out to be my redemption. I wanted to go so badly, I was dying for expression. I knew he was the only harmless access I had if I was to go so I started a pseudo-comeback campaign. I started talking about how we met and how I wanted to see him perform again. I subtly, yet persistently encouraged him to go for one of the poetry sessions. This one request seemed to sweeten him up. I was good, pleasing and deferring until he agreed. And what a day it was!

I saw my girls but stuck to Tega like glue. I dared not linger too long with them. But I felt liberated just by being there. Seeing the freedom the mic gave to people, juxtaposed against my entrapment caused a quake inside me. And I knew, I had to make a move. While he was per-

forming, my friends teased me about pulling an
inverse re-enactment of the last time we were all
there. When Tega finished, I gave him a standing
ovation and walked towards him as he left the
stage. He had a smug smile on his face as he
opened his arms for my complimentary hug but
the smile faded when he saw the look on my face
as I gave his hands a tight squeeze and walked
right past him to take the stage. I could hear my
girls hollering their encouragement and this gave
my chin a bit more tilt. I wasn't even sure what
to say but when my hands clasped around that
mic that night, its solid symbolism was like a
liberating embrace and my heart clenched into a
fist of pain as I began the sincerest freestyle I
had ever heard. It was an outlet of my anguish
and my fears. I could barely see through my tears
but my voice remained resolute to tell its story.
When I was done, my friends were around me,
holding me in a tight embrace, tears streaming
down their faces. I turned to my husband who
was by now sobbing shamelessly and I mouthed
the most powerful words I had ever said to him:
"No more".

*****

It's been three months since that night
and my life has taken a new bend. I and Tega are
currently separated and I am learning to unlearn
the fear he driveled deep inside me. But I am
worried for myself. I have been struggling with a

strange new pain. It is like the kind of pain left behind after holding a full bladder for too long and even after relieving yourself, you're left with an emptiness that hurts a little. A pain that comes from missing the thing that caused me pain. A dull throb that replaces the removal of a familiar pain. Maybe it is because I had gotten so used to having that pain in my life that I had grown around it, accommodated it. Or maybe it is because I am not used to living without it.

·g·

i remember
your swaggering gait
your beautiful twinkling baby eyes
your sweet spreading smile
the sound of your voice
and the train of your thoughts
your soft mouth, warm against mine
the taste of your kiss
the heat of your touch
the perfume-tinged musk of you

i remember
how my dear heart leapt
every time i heard the sound of your voice
how my skin tingled and warmed all over
at the trace of your fingers
how fireworks spiraled through my stomach
wall
setting butterflies shooting into technicolor
explosions
how the glow of your smile tanned my world a

golden hue
how i yearned to see the world through your
eyes

i also remember
the going
the silence
the wait
the long waits
no notes, no notice

silence

the long waits for the wait to end
the painful silence and the echoing distance
my poor heart alone
left out in the cold...frozen
while i cradled yours in the warm soft place
inside me where there were no hard things

i remember
the zigzags of uncertainty
my many resolutions and falters
the recycling of the same old scenarios

ololufe i'm getting too old for this
tired and weary of it all
and my poor heart can take no more

so right here is where i let go
here, i let your good go by
i've done enough for you
i've done too much for you
i've been too much for you

this i do for me
because i deserve me more than you do
fare thee well my first love

ipade wa, never more.

8.

Dilemma.

Dilemma

Tokunbo lifted me clear off the floor and I gladly wrapped my legs around his waist as he swung me towards the wall. My naked breasts and his bare chest kissed and I whimpered as searing sensations spiraled to my core from the contact. Pinned high against the wall, he ruthlessly took my mouth in his and my heart did a flip of joy. I love me this man. He's all the man there could be to a man. He can be gentle as a lamb, reverently taking off every piece of clothing I have on and softly nibbling at each layer of exposed flesh, taking his good ole time, making me quiver all over before he'd even begin to devour me. He can be amazing at quickies too, staying long enough to pleasure passionately, yet always driving home that climax. He can also be my fiery fierce lover. Tokunbo, my warrior. He could tear through layers of clothing in a blink, rough, yet all the way pleasing, biting here, teasing there, leaving a pleasure-trail as he pummeled through barriers of fabric to get to his prize. That's my Tokunbo, my man. I'm not quite sure which is my favorite of them all but then, who said I have to choose! I have them all in him.

But that day, he was being my fierce devourer and I was giddy with excitement. He'd been away for a week and immediately I saw him enter the room, I saw the fire of passion burning bright. After showering him with kisses and my tears of welcome, I nudged him toward the bathroom as he reached for the opening of my silk house robe.

"Oh no, not before you have a bath", I said as I pointed towards the bathroom.

He grunted as he pulled away and made for the bathroom but when he cast those baby-eyes mirroring his raw longing on me, I couldn't stop myself from gently tugging at the softly knotted belt of my robe to give him an eyeful of encouragement even as I walked towards him. He met me halfway and scooped my fun-size 5.5' frame against his hard 6.3', gripping my naked waist through the open robe. He placed me against him and I wrapped my legs around his waist. My naked stomach met his and heat spiraled through our frames as our breaths quickened and fingers fumbled over flamed flesh. He quickly tugged off his pants and was gloriously naked against me. I felt like a ballet dancer draped over her partner, as we started our special dance. It felt like the distance had been our rehearsal and this was our performance.

Dilemma

He kissed me with the intent to take beyond what was offered and draw out even more. He lowered his head and gently nipped at my breast and I whimpered. Deep laughter rumbled in his throat as he flicked his tongue at my nipple and I squirmed. When he finally took me into his hot mouth, I screamed. He teased and tormented my poor taut nipples, one and then the other, with his teeth and his tongue and his lips. Oh he wrought magic in me with those three messengers of his. And he still had more. I ground up and against him as I sought out his crown. He felt my hand searching and lifted his head, straightened his frame a bit and we came unseeing-eye to eye, yet seeing all there needed to be seen. He pinned my hands above my head as he sank into my welcoming wet warmth and swallowed my moan in his kiss. He kissed my lips, my ears, my neck, my breast as we rode on the waves of our special rhythm. My open robe was our cape, our passion was our super power. We took flight across the sky, to save each other through mindless pleasure. I tightened my leg-wrap around him and my fingers dug into his smooth hard back as we neared the crest of our joined waves.

My eyes rolled towards the ceiling, sending notes of gratitude to God for pleasure so decadent. That was when I saw him, standing there at the crack of the door, staring at us, his eyes clouded with something disturbing. But I was too far out in the thick of our cresting wave to care for our audience as we both let out mingling moans of sated pleasure as we peaked in explosion.

I looked at the crack of the door. He was no longer there.

Our skins gleamed with sweat and the room smelled like both of us. Tokunbo carried me to bathroom and we had a steamy shower (pun intended, *wink*) afterward and then I went downstairs to get my man something to eat.

*****

I pulled out a drink and closed the fridge, and he was standing there, behind the fridge door. I was surprised at the sudden company.

"What is it with you and snooping around?" I asked as I placed the drink beside the food on the tray.

He stood there, staring at me with that unexplainable disturbing look in his eyes.

"And what were you doing at the door earlier?" I picked up the tray but the sight of his massive boner threw me. My hands trembled in shock and I dropped the tray.

"Please make love to me. Please. Do me like you just did your husband. Leave me grunting like a wounded animal, grunting from the pain of your pleasure. I've always known there was a tamed wildness about you but that, what I just saw, please, do it to me, just do it to me once. Please!" He said, breathing heavily.

Dilemma

I stepped back in horror, my face heated with embarrassment and anger.

"What?! How dare you!," I spat at him. "How dare you insult me, insult us?! Can you hear the filth spewing from your mouth?! Do I look to you like a whore?! Hm-hmm! You better not let my Tokunbo hear you utter such dirt. My baby can be mad and when he's mad, he can be mean! If you're horny, grab an aphrodisiac and nail your wife until she speaks an unknown language. Don't you dare EVER repeat this. NEVER again!"

I grabbed the tray and stomped so hard up the stairs with the food tray rattling dangerously in my badly shaking hands, it was a miracle I didn't trip and fall in my blind fury. I stood outside my bedroom to catch my breath and try to calm down. How do I face Tokunbo with this? He always knows when something is wrong with me. I felt dirty. I must have another shower.

*****

I and my husband live in Malta. My best friend and her husband came to vacation here and since we have a pretty big house, we decided to host them. While my friend is sleeping off in their room, tired from an amazing day of soaking up the sights and sounds of Malta, her husband prowls, seeking his own destruction. This will really break her if I tell her because she just had a horrible miscarriage, the third in the past three years. They've had quite a rough year so far and she needs this vacation more than anything.

And when I tell my Tokunbo, let's just say, it won't be so great a vacation for anyone anymore.

What do I do now?

Shit!

.b.

why do i have to
be the one
to make a decision
about a choice
that i never made?

9.

Robbed.

Robbed

Sade was laying on the bed, staring blankly through the doorway. She was not looking at anything in particular but her brain registered movements through a fog. White blurry images walked past the door, again and again, coming to a halt at a spot across from the room she was in and then walked past the door again and again. She was looking but she was not seeing. When he walked by the door and came to a halt at that same spot where the white blurry images had often stopped, she knew it was him even though she could not see clearly. Her eyes simply stared vacantly ahead but her nose registered that familiar smell of him. There was some movement in the spot and the blur of him started walking towards her direction. Sade painfully rolled over and turned her back to the doorway.

She was glad that he was there to be with her. She really needed him. Yet she hated the fact that he had to be there in the first place, for the reason that he was. Two slow tears trickled down the cheeks as the pain-wave hit all over again.

She felt his presence softly fill the room

as he entered and she wished again that he did not have to be there.

He knocked lightly.

She tried to pretend to be asleep, to stall and delay the moment a little longer but her stupid nose decided to sniff oh so loudly at that moment.

He called out to her softly.

"Sade mi".

The softness with which he spoke her name seemed to break the dam of tears she had been holding back. Her frame jerked from the intensity of the sobs as they tore out of her. The pain seemed even way more painful than the pain of the incident.

He slid into the bed, cradling her gently in his strong arms like a little child while she cried like one. He whispered and crooned softly to calm her. She cried even more. For her. For what she had lost. For him. For what she had deprived him. For them. For all the times they fought the strong raging desire to give in. For all the physical aches they went through in their battle to keep their resolve. For their shared healing. For all the past battles they had won together. And for this one that had been stolen from them.

*****

She must have fallen asleep in his arms through her tears because she woke up in his amazing cuddle and snuggled even deeper into the spoon of his warm body. He was asleep too, or lightly dozing because his warm, light breathing gently fanned behind her ear. She moved a little and his hold tightened a bit more. She smiled softly. Even in sleep, he was always trying to protect her.

The thought brought back the ugly reality and she sighed heavily. He must have been woken by her sigh because he said softly against her ears, "Bad dream?"

"Not with you so close to me", she chuckled.

She sighed again and the tears brewed. She tried to fight them back, to retain that cocoon of peace with just the two of them in it but the tears slipped through her tightly shut eyelids and landed on his hand. He made to turn her to him so he could look into her eyes and soothe her some more but she pulled his hand into a tighter wrap around her. She just couldn't bear to look into his eyes. Not just yet.

"You don't have to talk about it now. The police called me already and told me what they know", he said. But she wanted to. She wished she didn't have to but she had to. And then too.

*****

"After you called, I planned to stay for just another 30 minutes because it was getting chilly and the waves were getting fierce and

distracting. I was almost done with the piece I was writing when this tall guy walked up to my little space. He smiled nicely and asked what I was doing. He was polite and sincere enough so I indulged him and told him I was writing. He apologized for disturbing but seemed curious to know what I was writing about. After a bit of insistence and since it was a surprise for you, I reckoned it couldn't hurt to show him and get the objective opinion of a stranger about it. So I showed him. He read through it, gave me a strange smile and said I must really love you. I beamed and nodded in agreement. He walked away while I finished up. Done, I knelt on my beach mat to pack up my things and then that same looming figure cast a shadow over me from behind. I turned around with a little smile to ask if he needed anything but the look on his face was rather strange. I couldn't quite place what it was but it sure was weird. He said the strangest words next and from thereon, things began to spin out of hand.

"I want what you have", he said.

I arched my left eyebrow in question and he bent towards my beach mat and tried to reach for me. I scrambled on my knees to the other end of the mat. It wasn't much of anything but it put a bit of distance between us. Something felt very wrong. I wasn't even interested in politely asking what he meant by his statement. I just wanted to leave. As I scrambled for my sandals, he dragged me back by my right leg. I toppled off my hand on which I'd been resting and fell halfway onto the mat. He tried to move closer but I quickly gave him my version of the 'SuperKick' in the chest. He said "that's rude" then the first slap came. Whack! across my face. He dragged me back to the middle of the mat. I mellowed a bit and tried to reason with him. I told him he could have what I had. It was all in my bag. My phones, money, everything. He laughed and said he wanted something in my bag quite alright. But it was my writing pad. But not quite. It was the poem I just wrote. He wanted my love. Our love.

I laughed at the ridiculousness of the notion but his next slap quickly washed it away like salt water. I was confused. I said that love was for both of us. Something we both felt for each other in our hearts. He retorted that love starts from somewhere and if I didn't give him, he was going to take it anyway. This set my head clanging and my vision blurred momentarily from the crashing beat of my heart. I started to thrash around and scream, hoping to break free and make a run for it but he held me firmly down, quite easily too. I felt helpless, like a piece of flapping rag in a windstorm and I began to break. He tugged at the fastening rope of my linen

pant and I thrashed around even more vio-
lently but I was no match for him.

He hurt me. Terribly. Horribly. He
hurt me. Beyond his blows and his slaps. He
hurt me with every shred of clothing he tore
off and every violent thrust. He hurt me
deeply but the worst hurt of it all, the very
cut that severed me was when he roughly
parted my thighs and forced himself into me.
He felt the resistance and was shocked. He
whipped his head up and looked at my face to
confirm the truth. When he saw the pitiful
plea in my eyes, he gave a loud whoop to the
sky and roughly rammed his way in. I
screamed. I lay there, numbing my mind but
feeling every single pain pummel through me.
My tears were hot lava from the erupting
crevice of my shattered heart. They were
burning tributes to my pain as well as our
love that he had sullied. Our love that he
made mockery of. I don't know when he fin-
ished. I just know I heard his loud animal
grunt in the corner of my mind I had crawled
into. I don't know how long I was laying
there, floating in the liquid numbness of my
mind when a kind woman and her little
daughter found me and called the police".

*****

His arms tightened around her as she
narrated the gory details. She didn't want to drag

him through the pain with her but there was no
way to relay the experience without going
through the motions. It was still too fresh in her
memory to wrap up in a summary. He spun her
around to face him and kissed her ever so gently.
He knew just how to make her feel better. He
knew that his kiss always worked every time but
the cut was too deep. She couldn't even kiss him
back. She tasted the saltiness before she saw the
tears on his face and it broke her a little bit
more. They both cried softly, their tears pooling
into their mouths as they swam through the kiss
together, trying to keep each other afloat.

"I'm sorry baby. I'll never EVER leave
you or let you feel any hurt again. I'll be here
with you, for you and I'll never let you go to any
hurt again", he said, each word tumbling out with
a sob.

She looked right into his eyes with all of
her heart in her eyes, pleading for the only
rescue from this nightmare she could think
about "Please make love to me", she pleaded.

He sat up, shocked. "What?!"

"Make love to me Cole. Please."

He held her away from him and looked
into her eyes, his mouth agape. She felt alone in
the cold in that moment of separation and he
must have sensed it too. He pulled her back into
his arms. She pulled back and held his face
between her palms. Looking deep into his eyes,
she said, "Take this nightmare away. Help me

erase this memory. I know you can. I know we haven't done this before. We never planned to until we are married but I know you can take this away. Please Cole..."

He looked dismayed. She was in dismay at herself too but she needed him to do this for her. It was selfish, she knew that. But she wanted him to purge her of this nightmare. She needed him to.

The tears came again and like two crashing waves, they both fell into each other.

.i.

and today, i am especially grateful for little miracles

like eyes not having fingers

i'm grateful that eyes don't have fingers
to slip past the protective pleats of my dress

i'm grateful that eyes don't have fingers
to slide between the folds of my flesh

i'm grateful that eyes don't have fingers
to crawl beyond the weak security of my hem

i'm grateful that eyes don't have fingers
to violate
with touch
this poor female body
which suffers so much violation already

i'm grateful that eyes don't have fingers

to reach and grope and tear
that which is out of sight

i'm grateful that eyes don't have fingers
because if eyes had fingers
if eyes were fingers
what an even more tragic world it would be
for the female body

10.

Two
Friends
&
A Bar.

Two Friends At A Bar

"Oh my! Oh my my! This is good! Oh this is really good!", she gushed. He beamed a satisfied grin and did a mock bow. He'd intended to knock her out with this one and it looked like he had definitely gotten her this time. He was pleased.

"I tell you Will, I've had some pretty good tries but this, mm-mm good! This right here is GOOD!" She took another sip and tilted her head backwards as if to manually transport the drink on its journey to her throat.

"This is the type of drink you slide back, not knock back. You see, you gently let it glide over your tongue and spread through your tastebuds soak as it slides along. Back there is where the magic happens. Your tastebuds burst into a colorful climax from the flirty caress of its fluid fingers. My word! It's amazing!" Her eyes glinted with excitement as she sipped and slid the drink once again.

Will watched her with great pleasure, beaming with pride. It was pure joy for him to see her so pumped about his creation and this

was a special cocktail mix he had made specially
for her to try out tonight. Lola was his friend, a
truly loyal buddy but a blunt one too, especially
in helping him inch closer to his dream of becoming a cocktail maestro. She was also a great
tongue to objectively measure his progress towards that dream. He had rarely ever seen her excited about one one of his creations but tonight,
this was definitely a good sign. Especially when
she used her special pronunciation of "good" to
describe the drink. That peculiar pronunciation
of hers was certainly a positive passmark.

As she took yet another "sip and slide" of
the drink, a guy approached the bar and ordered
a gin and tonic on the rocks. While Will turned
to serve him, the guy pulled a stool close to Lola
and said "Hi". And as always, her courteousness
to total strangers amazing him still, she respond-
ed with a nice warm "Hi" in return. Will loved to
watch the little dramas/exchanges between Lola
and the random guys who conveniently assumed
that a girl at a bar must be looking to get picked
up or was in dire need of male attention or that
they were doing a favor by walking up to her.
He marveled constantly at the simplistic vanity
of the lot of them but he was sure to enjoy the
outcome because Lola always made it a skit worth
watching.

This particular guy seemed nice enough
so it just might end in a little moment of polite
conversation over drinks. The thought had barely

formed when the guy right on reached out and squeezed out any prospect of niceness out of the evening.

"That looks like a rather fruity drink to be so excited about or to even be taken in a bar for that matter" he said. Will almost spilled the bottle of drink he was pouring. For the life of me, what sort of pick-up line is that?!!! He thought.

Lola slowly turned her head to look the guy in the face and Will stiffened. Oh-oh! This guy is so gonna get it!

Looking him in the face with a mischievous smirk slightly tilting the left-corner of her lips, she shifted gently, as if making to spin her stool to face him and her silence was interrupted by a loud rupture from her butt. She had positioned herself so strategically that it echoed against the stool to amplify the sound and bounced right toward the guy.

Will froze, his right hand hovering mid-air with the glass of gin and tonic.

The guy froze too as he reached for the drink.

And if the music wasn't on, the other people in the bar would probably have heard and reacted just as well. Lola on her part simply giggled and took another sip of her drink. Recovering from the shock, Will placed the drink in front of the guy who spluttered, "What was that?!!!"

Lola cocked a questioning eyebrow at him, motioned for him t hold on and with Will mouthing "Oh no" behind the bar, she gave another rendition of her unique dedication to the poor guy.

This time, he spilled his drink.

"That, was that. Like that, the first one was also that. The end". She beamed a goofy smile at him.

"What was that for, I mean why would you do something so disgusting?" he said angrily.

"What?! Why did I what?! Are you kidding?! THIS is my personal space. MINE! If you have a problem what i do within MY personal space, move on over man", she replied and then giggled naughtily.

"It's clear that fruity drink is obviously too strong for you. You better stop drinking and had home because it's obviously messing you up" he retorted.

"Excuse you! Slide off man!". She raised her glass of drink and tilted it towards him. "Cheers! Nah wait. No cheers. I really shouldn't be toasting this amazing drink to your tight-ass self. You can scoot off cheer-free". And she stuck her tongue out at him.

He grabbed his drink, arched an eyebrow at Will, who mouthed *"She's high. Sorry"* and with a last glare at her, moved to a different part of the bar to nurse his spilt drink and bruised ego.

"Well, well, you sure pulled off the fake high chic pretty well" Will said.

"Well he deserved it, mouthing off at this amazing cocktail of awesomeness and don't you even try to give me a hard time about the melodies I expressed because I'm not apologizing. After all, they didn't even stink". She took a slurpy long sip of her drink, staring at him over the rim of the glass with laughing eyes.

He chuckled.

"You are such a handful of quirky peculiarities and someone who doesn't know you would think you could not raise dust. My sympathies to those people who assume you can be leisurely dismissed"

"And that, my darling, is one of the few perks of this petite frame of mine" she answered.

"For such a petitie chic, you do pack a mean blast. Wow! The bass on that second one. Startling!"

They both chuckled.

"So...what are you going to call this one? And you better think up a cool name for it before you destroy the brand"

'I've not thought about that yet. I wanted to get the reviews be sure it in the big wide world"

'But of course it must make it out here. It just might become a house special in time" she said with an encouraging smile.

She gulped the rest of her drink, dropped her bill and grabbed her bag to leave. Will saw

the cash and started to protest but she held up
her hand to stop him.

"Don't worry, I didn't include a tip but
please do let me pay for this awesomeness. At
least, give me the opportunity to be the first
to buy it before it makes history. It was a great
treat".

"Alright then, if you insist. You take care
now". Enjoy the rest of your evening", he said.

"I sure will. Take it easy yourself", she
replied.

They bumped knuckles without actually
touching knuckles. This was their special buddy-
shake and they could do it even with distance
between them.

Will watched as she strode away, a soft
smile on his face.

His boss slid behind the bar and stood
beside Will, a mischievous smile on his face.

"When are you ever going to tell her?",
his boss asked.

"Tell her what?" Will retorted with a
slight frown.

His boss beamed a goofy smile at him,
wiggling his eyebrows in a teasing manner.

Pretending to return to work, Will replied,
"Sometimes, the existing love of a friendship
at hand is best preserved and preferred to the
promised love of a romance that is uncertain".

His boss cocked his head thoughtfully,
confused.

.j.

i hope you find the blessing of great friends
i hope you have friends so incredible that
when you're having a bad day,
you can scroll through your chat history with
them
and somewhere along that scroll,
you find such laughter
that makes you forget
why you were having a bad day in the first
place.

11.

Shroud
Of
Grief.

Shroud Of Grief

She shut her eyes tight, the crinkles around her eyes twitching rapidly from the effort. She snapped her eyes shut as she struggled to shut out the visions flashing before her eyes, hoping that perhaps, not looking would erase the harsh reality she had to confront.

The men who had come to break the news moved their shoulders in quick movements of disbelief that such a tragedy could (re)occur. With bowed heads, they struggled to keep their emotions together as they awaited her reaction. The eldest and spokesman of the group cleared his throat and she whipped her eyes open at the sudden sound.

"Is it true?", she asked as she searched the sympathetic expressions in the eyes of the men.

They could only answer with slow pitiful shakes of their heads as the group leader ran his right hand, slowly, up and down his chest in a calming motion, imploring her to take things easy.

She wondered why he was doing the calming motion when she felt so calm already. She also wondered at herself as well, how come she felt so calm? How could she feel this calm when she should be lashing her body to the floor in renewed pain?

She did feel pain, quite alright but rather than fight it, she allowed every pang of it to soak into her being. This pain was not completely new, it was more of a reinforcement of her previous pain. It was a new kind of an old pain. It was like having an injury, a very painful injury already on its way to healing and then suddenly tearing off the scab and tearing off the healing with it. But rather than scream out in pain, she sucked in the pain. This must be what it felt like when people embraced their pain. She had heard that it made the pain more bearable. Resisting or fighting it meant thrashing limbs and flailing arms and uprooted hair and painful bodily harm. This pain and the embracing of it brought with it a calm.

She raised her head and stared at the family picture up on the wall across from where she was sitting. Her two younger children were seated between her and her husband while the two older ones stood behind the chair, their faces rosy and smiley. Her children, yes, they were hers now, it sounded wrong but they were her children now and she was their only parent now. She had been left to bear alone the burden of two. All four of them were her children, all except her Ada who had gone to join her father barely one year after his heartbreaking departure. But come oh, her Ada's one year wedding anniversary should be in a few weeks and her husband's remembrance should be a few weeks short of that too since he died only 20days before Ada's wedding. She hadn't been able to attend Ada's wedding because of her widowhood rites and now she still will not be able to attend her anniversary or celebrate it because her Ada was gone too.

Now only four of them were left from that picture frame.

As this new reality painted its sad colors across her mind, and as the picture of her loss came into focus, a lone tear slid slowly down her cheek and plopped on her right arm. The gentle warm impact snapped her out of her thought train and she quickly wiped off the tear and its trail with her hand, willing it away, all the while wondering how it had gotten there.

The three men made rustling sounds as they prepared to take their leave. The silence, the calm acceptance was a change from what they had expected and it was slightly discomfiting but they welcomed the change from the usual stream of condolence words and sometimes, the physical exertion to restrain and calm the aggrieved. They stood to leave, dropping snippets of condolence here and again.

She looked up at them with a faint smile, wondering whether to say 'thank you' or 'goodbye'.

She nodded slowly, up and down, like the thoughts in her head were too heavy to shake too casually in a quick nod. She heard them give brief instructions to her eldest son on their way out.

She could hear the soft sobs of her youngest (now her only)daughter, Ogo, in the other room who must have been crying for a while now but she had been too engrossed in her revelry to hear. She could also hear the movements of people going in and out of the living room, speaking in soft tones amidst sobs.

She looked at her sister who had been sitting across from her all the while, tears streaming down her face.

She suddenly felt exhausted.

Casting a weary smile at her crying sister, she snuggled deeper into her grief.

.k.

june 23.

When you really truly immerse yourself
in the art of living,
you sharpen your senses to savor every second
and soak up every experience
into memory banks for the future.
And on those not-so-great days,
memory becomes comfort food for weary souls
and soothing salve for bruised hearts.
But conversely, the price you pay for really
truly living is that nostalgia sharpens
memory into a blade that cuts deep wounds
every time you remember your losses.
And then days like today salt the wounds of
memory and cause the many days of
healing to somersault into dust.
It still hurts like fresh wound, this loss of you
Ma Papa.

It still smarts like salt sprinkled on an ulcer
every time this day arrives.
Sometimes I forget that you are gone
and on those days, there are no pains.
But on this day, every year,
I am reminded that you
really are gone
and the pain deals me fresh blows.
You are often remembered
and always missed Papa.
You live on in me and my siblings
and all the people you crossed paths with.

We've made it through two years without you.
Here's to hoping we continue to make it
through the years that lie ahead with you as
our constant guardian angel and mediator.

Rest on Baami.

(in memory of my Pa, Mr. Samson Temitope)

12.

Sibling
Fight.

Sibling Fight

"Where are you going Titi? Come back here." Felix shouted at her back.

"Don't command me. You're not my master." Titi screamed back. She turned the door handle and peeked outside.

"You don't have any respect. How many times have I warned you not to shout at me? I'm your senior for God's sake!" Felix screamed back.

"And so? You're my senior does not mean you will now be controlling me! Are you the only one that will be someone's senior?" she shot back, pushing the door open wider and leaning further outside.

"Are you deaf? Where are you going? You're not supposed to open that door or go outside. Mummy already warned us not to leave the house." he said

"Stop shouting at me. I've heard. Did I go anywhere now? Am I not here?" Titi replied, angry that he had used the 'mummy' defense to get her to do what he wanted. She stood with the door open for a while longer, listening for his complaint so she could floor him.

"Why are you still standing with the door open?"

She slammed the door and zeroed in on him.

"What is it Felix? Why are you worrying my life? Every time, every time you will be stressing me."

"You called me Felix?" he asked, a look of shock on his pimpled face.

"Ehen? And so? Is that not your name?" she replied, her arms crossed over her chest, her weight resting on her left leg while her right leg tapped the floor in a continuous clap clap clap rhythm. This was her battle pose.

"How many times has mummy warned you not to call me Felix again but to call me *Brother* Felix? Am I your mate?" he asked, touching his chest and leaning forward with a frown on his brow.

"So because mummy has said I should be calling you brother now, that has now become your name abi? Even when mummy and daddy are not around, you still want to be claiming seniority," Titi said, rolling her eyes.

"You think I don't know all the sense you have been using to avoid calling me brother when mummy is around. You will walk from one end of the house to the other to tell me something when you could easily call me but because you are stubborn, you would rather come close to me to tell me than call me *Brother* from across the room You think I don't know? Well there's nothing you can do about it. I'm older than you and you must respect me," Felix said.

"And because you're *just* three years older than me, and it's not even complete three years. Two years and some months. Because of that you're feeling like you're my uncle, right?" asked Titi.

"Say anything you like. Mummy and Daddy have made the rules and I'll make sure you follow. If you like, go and buy the two years and some months from the market and add it to your age so we are the same age. Until then, you must call me brother. I'll forgive the one you just did. The next time you call me by just my name, I'll definitely report you. And you know what that will get you," he said wiggling his eyebrows up and down wickedly.

"If you like, be Granny Joe, if I don't respect you, I don't respect you. Period. Let me call you brother from now till tomorrow, it doesn't mean respect. And for your information, even if I call you brother, in my mind I call you Felix Navidad," she hissed and walked back into the sitting room.

He had been taunted with that nickname when he was younger and he disliked it greatly.

He clapped his hands in a dusting manner and rushed after her into the sitting room, "Did you just hiss at me?"

She pulled her lips together in a tight

squeeze and dragged out a long hiss. "It's my mouth and I'll do anything I like with it."

"You this girl, you are looking for my trouble this afternoon o. Who likes her should come and warn her o. I'll beat her o," he called out to no one in particular.

"Beat kor, beat ni", she replied, eyeing him up and down.

"Hey! The two of you better behave or no lunch for any one of you until Mummy returns. You can quarrel and bicker like bitter old bats all day long but if I hear any fight there, no lunch for anybody", called out a voice from the bedroom.

"But he..."

"But she..."

"Hey! Hey! I don't want to hear any stories. I've said my own." said the voice.

The two siblings eyeballed each other.

Titi looked at the clock on the sitting room wall. It was 12:15pm. She waited a minute.

"Aunty Ope, when is Mummy coming back?" Titi asked.

"I think around 4 o'clock or so" replied their elder sister from the bedroom.

"Okay."

The teenagers sat on the three-cushioned couch facing the TV, scooching far into the opposite corners of the chair, leaving as much space as possible between each other.

"Oh so you know how to call her 'Aunty'

right? Now that food is involved, you don't have a problem with respect, abi? Foodie!" whispered Felix, to avoid rousing the displeasure of Aunty Ope.

"Look at you. She is eight years older than me and five years older than you. She deserves the title. She doesn't have to force me to call her Aunty," Titi whispered back.

'Of course she doesn't. Just a simple food threat will always get you in line," he said and stuck out his tongue.

Titi flapped her fingers in front of Felix's outstretched tongue. He left it hanging out, his glaring eyes daring her to let her fingers touch his tongue. They continued like this for the next minute. When a drop of saliva threatened to roll off his tongue and onto the couch, Felix hurriedly retracted his tongue. Titi gave a whoop of victory.

"You should have let your hand touch my tongue. Then you would have seen what I would have done to you." Felix said, angry at the little loss.

"It's paining you that I respect her more than I do you." she replied and stuck her tongue out too.

'Will the two of you just shut up already?!!!" shouted Aunty Ope.

The teenagers chuckled conspiratorially at the frustration in her voice and quietly turned their attention to the cartoon showing on the TV.

Sibling Fight

.l.

This is your time
You are in your prime
Your strength is no crime
Sunny is your clime

Laugh out loud
Enjoy the sound
Forget your doubts
Be you and proud

Express yourself
Fear sure is hell
If you are in health
Then all is well

Love without disdain
Give without restraint
So long as your aim
Is still within gain

Make the best of all
Learn from life and move on
Look with hope to the dawn
You'll only be here this once

13.

Parted
Curtains.

Parted Curtains

I felt the chill today.

This morning as I walked to the stop to catch the bus to work, I felt the chill again. It was not the same chill I normally felt when I stepped out of the toasty warmth of the house into the cold of the early winter morning. It was not the type of chill that attacks the most lightly clad parts of the body, the parts that get gnawed at by the biting cold. It was not the typical chill caused by the driving winds of the old witch, Winter. It did not feel like a natural kind of chill. It was a chill that crept from the roots of the baby curls at the back of my neck and spread all the way down my back, making my stomach roil suddenly. A rush of goosebumps spread over my skin and my head seemed to swell in that weird manner my Mum believes is caused by passing ghosts. My heart thudded in sudden quick-steps and my eyes zeroed in on the window of house 2706.

The first time I felt that alien chill was last week Wednesday.

I was waiting for the bus that day as well.

As I always did, I stood right beside the STOP sign on the sidewalk on the intersection of Chase street and Terrivon road. I liked to stand there because it gave me a vantage view of the bus as it turned the tricky corner of Terrivon road and glided into Chase road. It reminded me of a great beast cautiously navigating its way through a fragile world, careful to reduce its destruction. That Wednesday, I was standing at my usual spot, my eyes fixed on that part of the corner where I'd catch the first peek of the bus and suddenly, the clouds opened up and cold icy drops of rain poured down on earth. With no chance to make the two minute dash back home without getting soaked and no bus shelter at the stop (thanks MTA!), I dashed to the front porch of house 2706. I was the only one out on the street, except for the occasional lone vehicle speeding through the pouring rain now and again. Most commuters did not get to the stop until mere seconds before the bus was scheduled arrival. And there was the one guy who catches the bus daily just as I do but who always seemed to step out just at the very moment when the bus is pulling away from the stop, running, arms waving and calling out 'Hold the bus!'

I pulled my phone out of my bag to check the time.

6:12am.

Five more minutes before the bus showed up. With the rain, I knew I was going to be alone till the bus pulled up for sure. I dug my hands deeper into my coat pocket and looked around the porch. It was a simple white porch with a big curtained window and a door that must have opened into the apartment at some point in the past. It must have been the main entrance since it was the front door but it sure didn't look like it had been used in a while. Its knob was a dirty copper and was mapped with rust and wear. The keyhole looked like it was vomiting rust and the peephole was blurred with age. It looked like a door that would groan loudly when it was opened. Or it could be the reverse; maybe one would groan from exertion if one tried to open it. I chuckled softly at this thought. I went and stood in front of the window and pulled out my phone to check the time again.

6:14am.

Three more minutes. Fingers crossed on that one, considering how messed up the bus schedules can be. As I tucked my phone back into my bag, a movement caught the corner of my eye. I turned towards the window. Everything was still. It was the most fleeting movement but it caught my eyes. There had been a slight movement in the folds of the curtain on the window. It was the slightest movement but I saw it. Maybe it was a gentle parting or a rustle, I wasn't sure but I knew I saw it. I moved just a bit closer to be sure. I wanted to see if someone inside the house was trying to talk to me, maybe chase me

off their property. At least, I wanted to know
how they felt about me standing on their porch
so early on a cold winter morning. I didn't want
any unpleasant surprises. The curtains didn't
seem to have changed from how they were when I
first looked around the porch earlier, except for a
slit of darkness down the middle of the curtain.
I looked through the slit but I did not see anything; neither through the curtains nor through
the shadows of darkness that intertwined the
folds of the curtain. Then I felt a chill. I pulled
my coat closer around me but the chill seemed
to increase. It spread across my body, kissing my
skin with bumps of uncertainty. It was certainly
not the kind of chill caused by the cold of the
morning because I was warmly tucked into my
coat. It was a weird thought but there seemed to
be something in the slit of the curtain beyond
my line of sight. I could not see it, try as I did
to peer into the darkness but my skin seemed to
be swarmed by waves and waves of chills. There
most definitely was something in that narrow slit
of darkness between the curtains. I had no idea
why I thought so but my curiosity was piqued.
My eyes roved and dug, unseeing, through the
slit, seeking what they could not see, yet seeking
still. I could see nothing but darkness as my eyes
probed and prodded, yet my skin told my eyes
not to tear away, speaking louder than my eyes
could see. There was something in there. And
it felt creepy. I wanted to pull away, walk away

from the porch and stand out in the rain if I had to. Maybe even make that two minute dash back home and to certain safety. I just wanted to get away from that chill spreading all over my skin in a creepy embrace. But I could not take my eyes away and my feet did not move. It seemed I was locked in place. I was not aware that my hand had moved until, out of the corner of my eyes, it came parallel with my face and moved onward still, reaching for the window. I was shocked. Not just at the sight of my hand moving without my control, but at my seeming inability to tuck it back into my pocket. My mind seemed to have lost control of my right hand and my left hand refused to move to drag its sister back to order. I felt like an external force was controlling my senses. My eyes refused to look away; my legs refused to move and my hands had turned rogue on me. My mind flittered with alarm at the thought of rogue. How could I possibly explain my innocence if my obstinate right hand reached the window? What was it going to do? What was I going to do? What was going on?

    I heard the hiss of the bus through the fog of my confusion as it rounded the corner and glided towards the stop, beaming its light my way. In that moment, it felt like an energy lifted off me and my frozen, rebellious senses eased right back to normal. I was unhinged from the claws of whatever creepy clutch I'd been in. My right hand lifted in a wave to flag the approaching bus as my feet kicked off in a quick dash to the stop. I jumped onto the bus, swiped my pass and sat down at a window seat, staring back at 2706 as the bus pulled away. My heart hammered against my chest. Not from the dash I just made to the bus but from the uncertainty of what had just happened and what could have happened. If I hadn't been wearing my glasses that morning, I'd have doubted what I saw next. But I had on my glasses and there was no doubt that I saw the curtains swipe back together suddenly, closing up the darkness.

I slid deeper into my seat.

*****

Today, as I walk towards my stop to catch the bus, that creepy chill is spreading over me again.

My eyes automatically swing towards the window of 2706.

Right then, before my very eyes, in a slow deliberate movement, the curtains begin to part and then, they stop, leaving a dark slit between the curtains.

It is the same slit in the curtains from last week. It feels weirdly familiar to recognize the slit.

I stop and stand right there on the sidewalk, chilled frozen.

.m.

shadows
graze the back of my neck
with a touch of nothing

14.

A
Baby
Changes
Everything

A Baby Changes Everything

There was a fevered excitement in the air. I could feel it as I drove into my street that evening. It was the type of excitement birthed by scandal and fueled by gossip. Frantic whispers hissed out of clusters of people scattered along my street. Whatever this gist was, it had spread through the neighborhood like harmattan dust in late December. I drove up to one of the clusters.

"What's going on?" Someone peeled from the cluster and answered, "Dudulewa is back from America."

"Yay! That's great! How's the baby?"

"Hmm that's why we are here o"

"Why?"

"Go see for yourself"

Was the baby deformed or sick? I wondered.

As I drove from cluster to cluster, the gist grew juicier. Some said she had slept with an oyinbɔ man and his seed had messed things up.

Others said the hospital had given her the wrong baby.

I was curious, yet hesitant because I didn't want to carry the dust of gossip into her apartment. Unfortunately, Sidi the busybody was visiting too.

"You're shining o Dudulewa. America did you good." Sidi said.

We both peeked into the tiny pink crib. Hair, yellow as palm-oil stain on white; skin, fair as warm milk and eyes, a riveting grey with hazel flecks. She was astonishing.

"Awwwwnnn! She's beautiful" I whispered.

"Wow! She's so white. You and Oga Abdul are stingy o, you both did not even dash her small from your dark complexion at all. She looks American. Or is it because she was born in America?" Sidi asked.

"No o," Dudulewa chuckled, "Abdul's great-grandfather was an albino and they said it re-appears in their family every fifth generation."

"Is that so?" Sidi said, catching my eyes with a wink.

I looked on unblinking.

.n.

Let us paint the world with our colors.
What if... just what if we were all col-
ors?
Imagine for a second that we were all
colors.
Seven billion distinct colors of us,
painting our way through life.

Imagine...

Imagine that as we navigate life, our
colors create a single trail that represents the
pattern of our journey.
Imagine that our differnet journeys are
mapped by our color.
Imagine, that we all start out as simple
primary colors. And as we meet one another,
our colors criss and cross, mix and match so
that no one color is primary because as we
meet one another, we take a bit of another's
colors.

Just imagine the beautiful super rainbows we would create together.

Now imagine, how life would be without all of our colors?

Imagine how much less beautiful the world would be if your color was missing. Or my color was missing. Or there was just your color. Or there was just mine.

Life is a canvas we have been given to paint together with our colors.

I hope you do not remain your simple primary color.

I hope you are colored beautiful shades and hues by the many amazing people you meet, taking a part of them and leaving a part of you with them, all of us a part of one another.

I hope you have experiences and create memories that deepen the hue of your color with character.

I hope the pattern your color draws on the canvas of life is not just a single line going back and forth, a single colored perimeter within which you box yourself.

I hope your pattern is a burst of wide curves and crazy tangled messy zigzags that become a magnificent abstract masterpiece of a life lived thoroughly.

I hope you take chances and leave familiar trails and zigzag through unfamiliar terrains and burst in your many different hues on to new roads.

I hope shades of your color are found in distant parts of the world, far far away from where you started.

And most importantly, I really really hope you leave a swatch of your color on the world.

Dear You,

life notes from me to you and me!

.1.

dear you,
Are you like me?
Some days you don't like the body
you wake up in.
You can't stand its scars and spots and folds.
And its weaknesses and frailties
and wrinkles and blemishes.
Other days you absolutely love this body
you've been blessed with.
You fall in love again with its curves and
sharp edges and valleys and hills.
And it's warmth and embrace and security.
And its strength and resolve.
And its changes and evolution.
And in this world of many strange things,
it becomes one of those things
which hold familiar comfort.
I hope you have more days when you love that
body of yours than days when you don't.

Dear You

Days when you can boldly say:

"No longer will I allow myself
To be ashamed of this skin
With its beauty and bruises
No longer will I be afraid
to wear this skin
Which covers me
Which warms me
Which holds my parts together
No longer will I reject this skin
Which I have known longer
Than anyone else has
Which I will own for longer than anyone's
opinion about it"

all my love,
toyosi

.2.

dear You,
Life is short.
But it is not all bad.
There are way too many beautiful
things happening in life to not #Live!
Seasons change and bring their differ-
ent forms of beauty with them.
Flowers are fairy children of plants.
Watermelon juice is joy and love con-
spiring in a cup to give you a bear hug.
My Indian colleague in America knows
Emmanuella, the funny Nigerian comedian
and she absolutely adores her.
My mother saying 'I love you' at the
end of our long distance calls is still one of the
best things to happen to me.
Warm blankets fresh out of the dryer
add a warm glow to cold winter nights.
Getting pushed around on an IKEA cart
like I'm reenacting a Jack&Rose Titanic scene
while shopping for cool furniture is mad fun.

Drinking garri ijebu with
milo and ice cold water
on a blazing summer day is da truth!
Being in love is beautiful.
Kissing is an absolute gift.
Music makes life better.
Babies smell yummy!
Reading stories about places that are
antipodal to your location
is wildly intriguing.
Using words like "antipodal"
is mildly satisfying.
Exchanging warm smiles with random
strangers is weirdly beautiful.
Jollof rice is still the MVP of all dishes.
The smell of rain kissing thirsty earth
is mouthwatering.
The sun shining bright at 9pm on a
summer night is eternally fascinating
and I absolutely love it!
The sight of light sprinkles of snow on
naked tree branches is breathtaking.
The sound of water sliding down my
throat makes me giggle.
The sound of my giggle
makes me giggle some more.
Life keeps happening. It simply won't
stop. And it is beautiful too.

Dear You

So don't wait to live.
Please.
Indulge your senses in active
intentional living.
Don't wait for a special day to wear
your favorite shoes.
Make every day special by wearing
your favorite shoes every single day you get.
We won't be here for forever.
Life is not forever.
LIVE!

all my love,
toyosi

.3.

dear you,
who lied to you?
who stole your truth and sold you a lie?

you were not made to blend
into the background
an aesthetic
for the eyes only
barely in sight
a bland backdrop

you were made to be a centerpiece
a force
an energy
gentle or great

you were made to be felt and seen
and acknowledged
who told you to alter yourself to fit a mold?

don't you see it?

you were not made to be anything but you

Dear You

you were not made to smell like flowers
or ice cream flavors
things that are easily waltzed by the wind
scattered in too many places to be great
you were not made from fleeting things
you were not made to be a passing fancy
lingering on the outskirts of the mind

no!

you were made to smell like rainy evenings
and dewy mornings and dark starry nights
a clinging petrichor both familiar and strange
all at once
hard to forget and easy to remember
you were made to leave a lasting taste on
hearts
a persistent aftertaste that many washes
cannot cleanse

you were made from things that last

you were made from the roar of thunder and
the strength of the earth
you were formed from the heat of the sun and
the power of crashing waves
you were wrought from the salt of the sea and
the mystery of dark nights
from the crest of high places and the dip of
steep valleys

Dear You

you were made from terrifying things

you were made to halt fingers in mid-caress
and bruise lips in kissing
to cause loins to burn bright with the
dripping oil of desire
to cause minds to race in wonder
and hearts to yearn in hunger
you were made to be a cause for study

you were made to be
absolutely
incredibly
beautifully
you!
don't forget who you are.

all my love,

toyosi

.4.

dear you,
Now that you're in college,
I hope you have the time of your life
Being in college is a time to learn yourself
As you learn your way to you
Remember to always stay true to you
Don't pretend to be what you're not
Don't fall into the trap of wanting to adult
too early

You've got magic
Don't throw it away because you want to fit
in
Follow your heart
Listen to it
Don't be a fool

Be confident without being arrogant
Be humble without being a doormat
You might feel intimidated or unsure some-
times
It's okay, you'll be just fine

Dear You

You might hurt sometimes and feel like you
will die
You won't die. You'll be just fine
You'll make mistakes and fail sometimes
It's okay, you'll be just fine
You will grow from these things

Don't stress over the failures of the past
Try not to be ashamed of your past
Without it you won't be where you are now
Savor the beauty of the present
Be grateful for the present
Not everybody gets to be present
in the present
Anticipate the promise of the future
Be excited about the future
It holds thrilling mysterious gifts

Allow yourself to be unserious
But don't forget to be wise too
Be carefree and don't worry

Learn to enjoy your own company
Sometimes that's all that will have
And all that will get you through messy
moments
Always make God the centre
Be grateful to the Maker
For blessing you with life

Allow yourself to fall in love
And to love deeply in friendships
College friends are usually lifelong friends
So don't be afraid to care deeply about them
and let them know that you do

Laugh out loud. Often.
Laugh at yourself. Often.
Never hide your smile
Dance in the rain
Forgive quickly. Apologize quickly too
Be generous with praise

Don't waste time on pointless arguments
Be content with what you have
You can make a lot out of what you have
Spend wisely
Go out. A lot.
Try new things
Have fun
Eat right
Some of the best experiences do not have a
price tag

Study hard
Enjoy the little things
Don't forget to add you to the list of things

Dear You

you love
And love yourself with deep devotion

Never lose your wonder
Nurture your inner child
Allow life to surprise you
Don't go through life feeling like nothing is
new or special
You'll miss out on the amazing moments
Go through life looking for that bit of special
in even the most ordinary

And please,
Read.
Read.
Read everything.

Don't just flow with the tides
Swim.
Dive.
Make a splash.

The world is yours
Go on ahead and be amazing!

all my love,
toyosi

.5.

Young girl
What do you see when you close your eyes
Where do you go when you are all alone
What do you want beyond what you've got
Where do you go to escape what you know

Young boy
What is your thrill
What is it that makes your heart skip
What is it that makes you rise up to face every
dawn
What is it that keeps your eyes dancing in the
dark of the night

Young girl
What is it you want to do
With this life that many so often lose
What is it you want to do
With this life you have in many ways
What is it you want to do with these lessons
you have learnt
What is it you want to do with these many

songs you have sung

Young boy
What is it that fuels your journey
What is it that mends your wounds
and keeps you going
What is it that unravels you
From the ball of defeat you so often curl into

Young girl
Where do you roam
Do you walk the corridors of the past
Do you explore the vista of the future,
Do you gaze unseeing into a vast landscape of
nothing and everything

Young boy
Do you know how to dream
Do you know how to free your imaginations
Do you know how to give your desires wings
Do you know how to make your thoughts sing

Set your dream free
Dream wild and dream free
Dream what you've never before seen
Dream in colors, rich and lush
Dream in details and dream again

Dream!
Dream your desire
Dream for better and better than you've ever
known
And far away places you want to go

Dream!
Dream of people and worlds unknown
Dream of learning and loving far deeper than
you know
Dream of food and culture and music all
strange
Dream of things without boundaries and far
out of your range

If you have ever been a dreamer
Dream some more
If you have never been a dreamer
Here you go
Get on with you

Dream new dreams and dream old dreams
Never be without a dream
In your journey you will go through things
And life will give and take from you
You will dream dreams that might remain
dreams

Dear You

And dreams that will waltz into the sun

This one thing I ask of you
That you never forget to remember your
dreams

The horizon doesn't end where you stop seeing
it...

all my love,
toyosi

My Humble Thanks

Thanks to everyone who has crossed my path on this incredible journey of life. You have added your colors to my rainbow.

Thanks to the amazing people who are the inspiration for the stories in this book. As you read and find yourself in these pages, may you find healing where it hurts and may you find joy where it sucks.

Thank you. Yes, You! Thank you for reading. Yes I 'm talking to you, dear reader. Lol.

Thank you Maami Owon. Abiyamo agboja gbanrangbanran. You are incredible. Your wit and wisdom is a soothing balm in a tough world. Baami lor un, I'll continue to miss you. Thank you for gifting me with your dancing shoes, your sweet spirit (yes! I'm sweet) and your love for reading. You live on in Jumoke and Joseph and me and Juwon and Jube.

Jumoke. Joseph. Juwon. Jube, what it do?!!! Lol!

Thanks to all my amazing friends, especially Benita Bulley, Eniola Johnson, KissDharmie (what's your real name again? Hahahaha I love you too Damilola Makanjuola) and Johanna Hammond for always reading my works. Hey KissDharmie, remember when you used to threaten to steal my journal and send my works to a publisher? I still hate you for that!

Thanks to Ifeoluwakiitan Oderinde, Victory Olaleye, Emmanuel Olutokun and Asabe Omogiafo for all the times you encouraged my writing. Of the many voices that encouraged me to keep writing, yours were consistent and resonant.

Special thanks to Aunty Joy, my primary school teacher (Learning Ground International School, Sari-Iganmu, Lagos) who put the first storybook (Ifeanyi and Obi) in my hands and set me on this path ever since. Thanks also to Brother Chuks, one of the first people to spark the dream of writing. I remember how you'd bring me novels and storybooks when I was a teenager and say "You can have them because I don't read all these books but I'm waiting to read your own book o." Here you go! I hope you enjoy it.

Thanks to all the people who borrowed (read: stole) many of my books in the past and never returned them. I still remember!

Thanks also to the people whose books I have borrowed (read: stolen) in the past and those whose books I'm coming for. Bless your kind souls. Thanks to all storytellers and writers who continue to add so much more wonder to life through the stories you tell. May your fount remain ever following.

Most importantly, thank you God for the grace and courage to start and finish this project. I spent many days deserting this book mid-writing but you always pulled me back. Thank you Lord.

all my love,

toyosi

this is my super kick to life's gut
(*apologies life, not literally* :-D)

it is my *"just do it"* move
my *"walk-on-water"* first steps
my mustard seed, tossed in the world
it is my clenched fist, jammed into the air
"for posterity and beyond".

•

•

•

i hope you enjoyed it.

all my love,

toyosi

Let's Write Together!

Wanna join me in this playful writing
exercise?
No pressures!
Nothing serious.
I promise.
Just your thoughts expressed in your words.

You down?
I hope so *fingers crossed*.

Okay.

There's a writing prompt on the next page which
I think will be fun to respond to.

I'd absolutely love to read your response!

Try to describe the sensation of beauty.
Stuff beauty into your senses and try to
express the sensation in words.
How would you describe beauty according to
your senses- taste, sight, smell, sound and feel?
What are things that you have tasted, smelled,
heard, seen and felt that you would use to
describe beauty?
How would you describe the taste of beauty?
The smell? The sound?
What would beauty feel like?
What does beauty look like?

I hope you do it!
If you do, *oh please please please* share
snapshots of your response with me on:
Instagram: @towyoursea; @dearyoumusings
Facebook: Toyosi Elizabeth Temitope
Twitter: TowYourSea
Email: toyosi.temitope@aol.com
Website: www.toyositemitope.com

Beauty